Has Anyone Seen My Daisy?
The Second Time Around

By
Peggy O'Connor

PublishAmerica
Baltimore

© 2007 by Peggy O'Connor.
All rights reserved. No part of this book may be reproduced, stored in a retrieval system or transmitted in any form or by any means without the prior written permission of the publishers, except by a reviewer who may quote brief passages in a review to be printed in a newspaper, magazine or journal.

First printing

ISBN: 1-4241-8704-4
PUBLISHED BY PUBLISHAMERICA, LLLP
www.publishamerica.com
Baltimore

Printed in the United States of America

Introduction

Kevin was only three and wandered in front of some people. When he turned, he did not see me. "Has anyone seen my Daisy?" He frantically scanned the faces in front of him, a sudden look of fear on his little face. I called out and stepped around the people so he could see me. He grabbed my hand and said, "I didn't see you!" I explained the importance of staying close, but knew that this would happen again, because he was such a curious and gregarious child. He had started calling me Daisy when he was only a little over one. Each night I would sit and play with him with a bright and cheery "Daisy Duck" hat on my head. It had huge eyes with large lashes and a giant pink bow on top. He would pull the beak and say, "Daidy, Daidy Duck." One night, as I walked in, my husband said, "Kevin, look who's here! Kevin ran to the top of the stairs and yelled, "Its Daidy, its Daidy Duck!" I remained Daisy, until I became Mom.

Ring, ring
Hello, goodbye,
It's so nice to hear your voice
The chatter of love and friendship flows musically over the wires
It's been so long, we really should keep in touch
I was thinking of you and thought I'd give you a call
I love you, I miss you,
Dad, I need some money
Mom, send cookies, I'm hungry
I'll be home for Christmas. Meet me at the airport
Ring, ring
This is the call a doctor hates to make.
There is something there. Tumor, Cyst, Surgery?
Goodbye. I really cannot talk right now.

It was a cool, sunny day in early May. Just days previous, we had journeyed home at high speeds, fear our companion. The hotel had sent for paramedics. I could not even remember the letters of CPR, let alone perform the tasks of breathing life into her. As her breath came to an abrupt halt, I exhaled my life, as my firstborn lay her head in my lap, just moments after suffering a seizure. We sped home, switching drivers, catching a few winks at rest stops, drinking cup after cup of coffee to combat the fatigue that threatened to slow us down. Our single goal was to get her home to our doctors and our hospital where she would be well cared for. Get her home. Find the answer. What caused the seizure?

We had arrived in Florida on Thursday. On Friday, she had her final review with her supervisor. She sat on a bench by a fountain in Epcot in the warmth of the Florida sunshine. She was so full of dreams. She was going to change schools where she could focus more on fashion and felt her experience with Disney would be a great asset to her resume. The rest of the day, we spent moving her out of the college housing and into the motel with us. She kept teasing Colleen, giggling and laughing, so happy, so secure. That night, she became somewhat moody, saying she did not feel well, she had "gotten her period," a quite normal occurrence. We went to bed, readying ourselves for the drive home the next day. About 8:30am on Saturday, Colleen spoke first, "Cut it out Kathy." I took a small peek through a narrow opening of my eyelids. Sisters together again, were poking at each other. Again, Colleen rebuked Kathy to stop fooling around. Pat started to get up to see what was going on and I said, "Ignore them, they're just goofing around." Colleen jumped out of bed and said, "What I want to know is why is Kathy shaking like that?" We both leapt to our feet and looked at the adjoining bed where Kathy was face down on the mattress. At first, we both thought she was laughing. She was like that, a practical joker, who greatly enjoyed laughing at the results of her jokes. When I looked the second time, it hit me, "No she's not, she's having a seizure." I picked up the phone to call the desk for help. They were slow to answer so Colleen fled to the door and ran across the pool area to the lobby to get help. The phone connected as she arrived at the front desk. I told them we needed the paramedics. They told me we probably did not need the paramedics and they could take her in the van. I firmly stated, "I WANT the paramedics!" Pat and I sat on the edge of the bed and rolled Kathy over, placing her head in my lap. It was a frightening moment when she stopped breathing, which we found out later, was normal at the end of a seizure, when they stop breathing for maybe a minute. This was the longest minute in my life as I stared helplessly at Pat, not even able to remember the letters of CPR, let alone what to do.

The paramedics arrived and called ahead to bring her to the hospital. It was a frightening moment when I asked them where they were taking her. Their conversation consisted of whether it was an odd or an even day, as that would determine what hospital she would go to. I firmly told them I did not care the day of the week; I wanted her taken to a trauma center, not an E.R. They argued that she did not need a trauma center. Pat went in the ambulance with Kathy while Colleen and I stayed back and got dressed. I remember looking at Colleen sitting on the edge of our bed as everything was happening and noting that her skin was as white as the sheets. It had been a trauma for her too.

HAS ANYONE SEEN MY DAISY?

When Colleen and I arrived at the emergency room, (They had ignored me and not taken her to a trauma center.) we found bedlam. The nurse, who was obviously very competent, was caring for a patient with cardiac arrest from another hotel, Kathy, and a few minor cuts and bruises. My mouth fell open as the doctor came out of the men's room, in scrubs and gown, yawning and scratching his genitals. Confidence in this place was not prevalent. The nurse, we found out, was going into her third shift without relief. She was on the phone, trying to get someone to relieve her, without success. After a preliminary examination and an x-ray of her head, the doctor wanted to admit her. We said no, we wanted to get her home to our doctors. He prescribed anti-seizure medication and we had to sign consent that we were taking her out against medical advice. By the time we left the hospital, Kathy was tired, but more alert. We returned to the hotel to pack our things in the car and pick up Kathy's sorority sister whom we were to drop in Indianapolis. How did we get here, to this place in our lives? I live it over repeatedly and get no answers. We crowded everyone into the car, with the memorabilia gathered in the past four months. Our drive was filled with trepidation as the question of what could have caused Kathy's seizure filled our minds. We could not admit to the depth of those fears, a brain tumor. Tension filled the air in the car as we sped home in anticipation of finding the answer. Sleep enveloped our passengers. Pat and I exchanged driving, catching a few winks when we could. We were both exhausted from the physical demands of the past day and the grueling drive of the past 12 hours. The thought of stopping at a hotel, wasting precious hours, was not considered. We just could not give into our physical need for sleep. Our well-being, our needs were just not high on the priority list. There was only one thing on our minds. Get her back home and find out what was wrong. The fear of the unknown was consuming us. She was ready to return home, finish school, and get a job. However, we knew all too well that we could not ignore the seizure. Something was wrong, very wrong. We wanted answers but were afraid to hear them. We were also confident we could handle whatever was in the future for us. Together we had the strength of an army.

I remember so well the night she called to tell us she had been accepted in the Disney College Program. She was so proud and so happy! We only had about two months to plan for her trip and she would be in Florida for almost four months. She had contentment about her; maturity was creeping into her life. She was 20 years old and planning her future like most girls her age.

The day we put her on the plane, I returned home to start a three-day crying jag. I cried all day Saturday, cried over the pancakes I made for Sunday breakfast, cried over Sunday dinner and on into Monday. When I finally stopped, Colleen asked why I was crying and I replied, "Because I'm so happy for her." It was true. My first-born had grown up and left home. While I was happy for her, it was time to mourn a part of my life which was now over. I did not, could not, anticipate that there would be more tears to shed within months. I anticipated nothing but happy things for my beautiful daughter. Life was hectic. Pat and I were both working full time. Colleen was in high school and Patrick was working and going to school.

In March, Pat flew down on business and spent some time with Kathy. In April, during spring break, Kathy called to say she was sick. She had asked to be relieved early because she was sick, and had collapsed on the bus taking them back to the college housing. They took her to the emergency room where they diagnosed a cold and flu. She got sicker and her friends took her back to the E.R. where again they diagnosed a virus. Colleen and I flew down to visit her for a weekend in April, returning home to await the planned trip two weeks later to bring her back home to suburban life. Kathy was enjoying the festivities and being with her many new friends from various states, like Monorail Matt and many other colorful characters. Now, here we were. I continued to hold my breath, in fear of losing it all if I allowed myself to inhale and exhale normally. I so wanted to think positive, but fear consumed me. I would lie and worry at night, sleep escaping me. Pat was able to let it go and drift into a peaceful sleep. How could he do it? Day after day, I went through the motions of life. Taking care of job and home were my usual routine. Now, visiting the hospital would become an everyday occurrence in my life.

Hurry, hurry, before it's too late
There are things to do
People to see
Questions to ask
Answers to hear
Hurry, hurry, and do not be late
Time is of the essence
We cannot wait!
Answers we must get
Our questions will not go away
Now we must hear the answers
Before it's too late

After admitting her to the hospital, we returned home and dropped into bed out of exhaustion. The next morning, tests were begun. Pat and I reported to work waiting for results, hoping that pursuing our daily tasks would somehow keep out anything terrible. I spoke to Kathy on the phone a few times and she was going about the whole process with her newly acquired "Disney" attitude, positive and cheerful, stating everyone at the hospital thought it was nothing serious but they needed the tests to confirm that. We all went to see her that evening and by then her room had begun to take on a party atmosphere. She had called a few friends to say she was home from Florida and in the hospital and that started the ball rolling. The fear that had consumed us on the ride home was put on the back burner. Nevertheless, putting it there did not diminish the concern we had over what had been serious enough to cause a seizure. We had no answers or guesses as to what it could be. Brain tumor was not yet in our vocabulary. As we waited for the test results, we thought perhaps this could be a cyst, not a tumor, on her brain and had something to do with a previously diagnosed syndrome. We thought back. Did we do something wrong in raising her? Did we overlook something? We worried because Kathy had been sick a lot when she was young. You cannot help but wonder where you went wrong. You seek a reason or logic, where there is none. Kathy ran high fevers as a toddler. She got strep throat every year without fail. However, nothing had been serious enough for hospitalization except her surgery at age 16. We noticed a small lump on her hand when she was just four. We went through the doctors and specialists and found that she had an unusual syndrome that caused the bones in her hands and feet to grow very thin with cysts inside them. The largest was on her left hand. The doctors decided not to operate because she was so young and the area of bone affected was at the growth line. Surgery at that point could cause a problem in the growth of her hand. They decided observation until she was finished growing. We paid little attention to this as she grew. No pain, no symptoms, no worry. When she was sixteen, she fell while on a ski trip and broke the bone. New doctors and hospital dictated that it was time for surgery. Healing was complete and there was no worry about the future. It was possible for one to occur in other areas of her body, but they would watch her for that. The Orthopedic doctor who had performed the hand surgery was called in for a consult and confirmed that whatever was on her brain had nothing to do with the previously known condition. In retrospect, I wonder what we thinking. We both knew my dad had died of a brain tumor and knew the occurrences in his life prior to his death, which were later identified as symptoms of the brain tumor. However, he was not diagnosed until after his death. He died on the operating table during exploratory surgery looking for a tumor behind his liver, which was what all his doctors considered he had. It was only in autopsy that they found the brain tumor which caused his death. There were no CAT scans then and people usually died quickly after diagnosis, if not prior to it. Brain tumors meant death, and soon.

On Tuesday, we each left for work, following our usual routines. Pat said he was going to leave work early to go visit her in the afternoon, as he had the day before. I had stepped out for a quick lunch and walk before returning to accomplish my afternoon's duties before going to the hospital myself. When I returned from my lunch break, the office was quiet, as everyone else had not yet returned leaving only a few inner offices occupied. As the phone rang, I answered with my usual greeting, only to hear our doctor's voice. "Mrs. O'Connor, this is the type of call a doctor hates to make. There's something there and we need to get it out." I felt my body slump in the chair as I held my breath in fear of confirming what I had heard by exhaling. NO! NO! Were the words in my head, but I could not get them out of my mouth. The doctor continued, "Do not tell her today. We will meet tomorrow morning with the neurosurgeon and we will all tell her together. Going along with this turned out to be the biggest mistake of my life. Until her death, Kathy had trouble trusting me to tell her everything. We had always demanded to hear everything up front, and had always taught our kids that knowledge was the best way to battle anything. If you know what you are facing, you can learn how to fight it. I immediately tried to reach Pat at work and then at home without success. I thought I might get Colleen at home, but I could reach no one. We did not have cell phones then. I could not call the hospital without alerting Kathy. I acquiesced to the doctor's request and did not tell her.

Kathy's college major was in Fashion Merchandising which meant sewing and design were a big part of her studies. She had asked me to pick up a pattern book from the sewing shop so she could review some projects she had in mind as she sat in the hospital awaiting tests. I determined that I must act as if everything was normal. I left work early and stopped at home in another attempt to find someone but found the house eerily silent. I stopped at the sewing shop and picked up the book she had requested. As I walked into her room, the atmosphere was full of laughter and friendly chatter. Pat and Colleen were already there and all were engaged in their usual bantering and teasing. I kissed her and handed her the book. She was so excited to get it, complaining that it was boring sitting in the hospital all day. She had made friends with her roommate who, by now, was engaging in the friendly chatter with us. I was the only one in the room who knew what was coming. I wanted to scream! Instead, I just stood at the foot of her bed, taking in the laughter, admiring how good she looked, tanned, good muscle tone, and an attitude that would send the worst pessimist on their way! I prayed to God, pleading with Him to allow her to survive. If only she could live at least long enough to be married and have a child, to fulfill the dreams that most young women have. I never anticipated that those prayers would be answered so literally! When we returned home that evening, I sat Pat and Colleen down and told them about the call. The guessing, the denial, was now over. There was something there to confront. Our only hope now was that it could be a cyst, not a tumor, and the surgery would define that. The next morning we arrived at the appointed time and the neurosurgeon did his exam, asking her to walk, scrapping a needle along her arm, looking into her eyes, asking questions. He then told us that surgery was necessary, that there was something there, and they needed to find out what it was. He saw no reason for waiting and scheduled her for the next morning. When Kathy found out I had known the day before, she was angry. "Why didn't you tell me Mom? You would have expected me to tell you if our roles were reversed." She was right. What could I say? The words I am sorry filled the void, but did not erase the trust that had been stolen.

The following day, we arrived early to be with her prior to the surgery, knowing she would be scared. We walked with her as they rolled the gurney down to surgery. She had been so hyped about her Disney training and shared so much about the challenges that Walt Disney surpassed before he actually succeeded. I bent to kiss her and whispered the words she had been living by, "When you wish upon a star, your dreams come true." About an hour later, the surgeon came to update us. There was a blood supply to the tumor, which meant it was cancerous. He saw no reason to wait and asked for our permission to go ahead and remove it. Up to that point, there had not been a moment in our lives as serious as this. Our first born, a beautiful, bright, and happy young woman, who had the rest of her life to look forward to, was going to have a brain tumor removed. She was not even 21! The surgery went smoothly. Brain surgery is the easiest they told us. There is less bleeding, fewer traumas to the body and recovery is usually quick. We went to intensive care when she was moved from recovery. Her head was enveloped in white gauze, her beautiful, full chestnut locks shorn and lying on the floor of the surgical room.

Kathy's best asset was her beautiful blue eyes and long, curly lashes. Even as a child, everyone would comment on them. As she awoke, I noticed that the deep blue had replaced the gray I had noticed weeks ago in Florida, which had evidently been caused by some pressure from the tumor. The white bandages made her eyes more beautiful. By dinnertime, she was begging for food. By the next day, she was literally bouncing on the bed, begging us to bring her a strawberry milkshake. She was transferred to a room to await the results of the biopsy which would take several days, three at least, maybe a week. Waiting that long was stressful for us all, but we wanted it to be right. We clung to the hope that perhaps they would find it was not so bad. One of her boyfriends came to visit her. The Memorial Day weekend was coming up, and he wanted to take her to Great America. She felt fine and wanted to go. She begged the doctor, who stood with his mouth agape at her request to go on the roller coasters. He finally agreed to a weekend pass, but no roller coasters! The fear and anticipation that was felt just a week earlier was replaced with joy as she came home. We had no prognosis, but were hopeful. Two boyfriends were waiting on the front steps as we returned home and she brought them in to visit. She pleasantly allowed herself to be wrapped up in the attention. She was a typical young girl, visiting with old friends and talking on the phone.

A young girl's life
Hangs in the balance
Beauty beholds her
So young and so lithe
Illness attacks her
Removes the façade
Of youth and beauty
The fine line of happiness
Threatened to break
Dreams, plans, forever to wait
Treatment, nutrition, become the priority
Begun in the surgical suite
When locks of chestnut brown hair fell to the floor
Radiation, chemotherapy, prognosis
New words in her vocabulary
Never to be gone

Pat and I had worked as a team on this, me taking care of physical needs at home and at the hospital; him leaving work early to go the library to research brain tumors. He had come home after three days of research when I finally got the courage to ask him what he had found. He slumped, as he said that the first two days were not good, prognosis was bad in general. However, he had noted that the dates of the articles were old and asked the librarian about that. She offered to contact Northwestern University Medical School for the latest information on brain tumors. It was only in the previous year that they had made leaps and bounds and prognosis for brain tumor patients had improved tremendously, especially in young adult patients. We had a battle, but a battle we could fight. Eventually, the news came. It was a tumor with different components, some of grade two and some grade three, out of a possible four. Radiation and chemotherapy were the plan. When the doctor came in to tell us the results, I thought "damn, here I am, alone again, to take in this information." I needed Pat to hear it too and to help me understand. He had been doing all the reading. However, I was not about to tell the doctor to wait. We needed to know. Questions could be asked later. The doctor wanted to start on radiation immediately. We agreed, but there was still a question of chemotherapy. Our neurosurgeon and his partner said no to chemo. The oncologist recommended it. Knowing the devastation of both treatments, we were concerned, but wanted Kathy to have the best chance to survive. We wanted her to live! Pat was able to contact several doctors involved actively in the treatment of brain tumors and a conference call was set up between a hospital in California, a university hospital in Chicago, and our doctors. We had the top doctors on the subject of brain tumors on this call. The result of all this was not definitive. The neurosurgeons all agreed that they probably had gotten it all…wait and see. The oncologists all agreed, why wait? She is young and healthy…be aggressive…don't take any chances. The decision was up to us. The greatest minds in this field could not make the decision for us. We went to Kathy and this time, told her everything. She decided to go with radiation, followed by chemo for one year. She, nor we, understood what that decision would entail. We knew all too well from Pat's parents and my sister that radiation and chemo would be rough. Kathy was strong and could handle it. Could we be the support to meet her needs? We were blind to the future. We just wanted the desired outcome to be the result. We so wanted our lives to return to normal. Kathy was a beautiful young woman. What would these treatments do to her? She was upbeat about it now, but what would happen when she began to wear down from the massive attacks on her body of the chemicals that were to save her life.

The secondary part of this decision was the rest of the family. When a serious illness hits, it affects everyone, not just the afflicted one. We would need more help from Patrick and Colleen to accomplish this. Kathy would need to be transported to the hospital and then the doctor's office to get the treatments. The treatments would make her tired and sick. She would need us to make sure she ate and drank enough fluids. She would need us to help her understand what was happening. We would not have time to do the many household chores needed to keep the house running. Pat would not have time to cut the grass, change the oil on the cars, or do repairs when needed. We needed to depend on our family for that. Nevertheless, this placed a tremendous burden on Patrick and Colleen. There was really no choice. We had to try to save her life. That was the priority. We were literally at the mercy of anyone who could help us.

The answers are in
We don't like what we hear
We are ready to fight
We will not give up
She has a battle ahead of her
But we will be there
We will stand united
She will survive, by golly
She will survive
Please God let her survive

Once the cards were on the table, it was up to us to plan. We did not want to waste time so we followed through on starting radiation treatments. For extended treatments like chemotherapy, it was time to get second opinions, educate ourselves on latest treatments, and psych the family up for the battle. We were looking at over a year dedicated to her treatments, hoping that additional surgery would not be needed.

The fight begins. Her radiation treatments started the following Monday. She took the first few treatments as an inpatient before being released to continue as an outpatient. The bandages were removed, showing the scar on the right side of her head. Her hair had already begun to grow back and she was optimistic that she would have a full head of hair again. The radiation treatments left her tired and weak. The sparkle in her blue eyes diminished as the rays attacked the cancer cells. She still tried to joke and laugh, but the luster was worn off. She was so young to be fighting this battle, so full of life! How unfair! How could God allow this to happen? Always my prayers were for happiness, good health, and enough to pay the bills, with a little left over for fun. I had not asked for the world…just enough. Radiation treatments lasted six weeks. She had been inquisitive about the different types of rays used to treat her. How were gamma rays different from beta rays? She celebrated the last day by bringing "gamma baby" cookies to the nurses. They were sugar cookies, shaped like little blobs and frosted with blue and pink frosting. The night before her last treatment, we came up with the idea of the cookies. Kathy immediately went into her usual manipulation to get me and Colleen to do the baking. We all got silly, joking about the cookies. Colleen was adamant that if she were going to bake, Kathy would have to help. Therefore, Kathy obediently asked what she should do. Colleen said, "Beat the eggs." Kathy proceeded to do as she was told and literally smashed the eggs on the counter. The comedic relief was welcomed as we laughed until we cried. When the cookies were done, we all retreated to the basement family room to shelter from an impending storm with tornado warnings. The dramatic change in the weather seemed an ominous signal of what was yet to come.

I vowed to make a deal with the devil if that was what was necessary to save my daughter's life. Pat prayed that God take him and give her youth and vitality back where it belonged. Everyone prays this way when his or her child is in any kind of trouble. However, we forget it is not up to us. It is up to Him. We, as believers, must find a way to deal with it. We pray for His help. I have called on that help so many times. Someone gave me the Footprints prayer card where God is carrying the man when he could not walk, inferring that God is always there, even when we think He is not. Believe me, there were times when I wondered, there were times when I was angry with God, and there were times when I was humbled after some little miracle occurred to bolster my belief. My mother had always taught us to have a black dress in the closet, just in case we needed to attend a funeral. One of my first decisions after Kathy came home, was to throw out everything I owned in black and replace it with bright, cheerful colors. I would affirm Kathy's attitude to beat the cancer. I read books about survival, self-help books, and prayers and talked with anybody who had any knowledge on the subject. Armed with knowledge, we could fight.

A New Lease on Life
I have won!
I beat the enemy!
I will forge on
To better things
I may be weakened by the battle
However, my resolve is stronger than ever
My dreams were put on hold
My hopes flashed out
Nevertheless, the fire in me relights
I will succeed
I have survived

C is for Cancer

June 1990

These words are for you Kathy. Keep up the fight. When you get tired, look for strength in me. For when you are weak from treatments, I will be strong. I know I cannot take the physical pain and weakness away from you, but remember in your mind and heart, that I am there to give you strength. Yes, I will expect a lot from you because I intend to treat you like a survivor, not a failure.

Now I've learned my ABC's….that childhood song is so familiar. Now I am forced to learn a new alphabet, one, which describes how my life has changed since my daughter, was diagnosed with cancer. Whether it is the patient or their loved one, their lives are changed forever, suddenly and with dramatic finality. We live in fear of cancer and most of us try to deny its' very existence, until for some of us it becomes a reality, whether it be ourselves, or a loved one. Then we are forced to confront the reality. It is a disease, which takes so much, from the very cellular makeup of the patient to the emotional upheaval of everyone around them. It is not selective to young or old, male or female, married or single, widowed, or retired. It does not care. The universal cry is "WHY ME?" There is no answer. However, today there are many battlegrounds where cancer is being fought and it is for those fighting the battle that I offer these words. Don't give up. You have only just begun the fight!

A Is For Anxiety

God, I am so scared! I try to be brave and keep a smile on my face, but sometimes, it is so hard! Please Lord, stay with me, and give me strength in the bad times to be positive and put a smile on my face. I know I will feel better if I do. There is plenty of time to cry and feel bad, so help me to make the times for feeling good increase in number until there are more good times than bad.

B Is For Bravery

So many people tell me I am so brave. I am not. I am scared. I do not want to be brave because I do not want to be in this fight. I just want to be me and do all the things I usually do, and fulfill the goals I have set for myself. Nevertheless, I guess for now, I should acknowledge that I AM brave, that I am different than I used to be, because now I am a soldier fighting a battle. Perhaps I should wear my battle scars proudly for I am a winner!

C is for Cells

They say that cancer is cells gone crazy. They do not know why these cells grow this way. They just do. But cells are my very existence! After all, what am I but a composite of cells? Babies are made by cells dividing and growing and look at how beautiful babies are. They say we have good cells and bad cells. Well, from this point on, I am going to denounce these bad cells within me because they have no power over me because I will not let them. They may go to hell with Satan for all I care! I promise that I will work on my good cells and give them every bit of my energy so they may win this battle for me.

D is for Disease

I now have a "disease." That sounds formidable! How should I feel about having a "disease?" My disease is famous and intimidating. The spoken word scares people like it used to scare me. Help me to remember that this "disease" is only part of what is happening to me. I am still alive and while I must give much time and energy to this "disease," I will not let it rule my life for I am in control!

E is for Energy

Oh, it takes so much energy to fight! My body gets tired and my mind gets sleepy from all the drugs I must take for this battle. Lord, please give me the added burst of energy I need. I need energy to survive treatments. I need energy for my family. Sometimes, it takes all my energy to smile!

F is for Fight

Because I intend to fight! I will not sit back and give up my life, for I have so much to live for! I have my loved ones who need me. I have a job to do. God put me on this earth for a reason and I do not intend to give up and not finish the job. I intend to stay and fight to complete my job so when I do go before God, He will say "good job, well done."

G if for Goals

I am going to set my goals. The first is that I will survive. The second is that I will get through each treatment. The third is that I will make every effort to be what my family needs me to be. I will be patient. I will not get upset because people do not know what to say or what to do. I will try to understand that they mean well and that they are hurting as much as I am, maybe more, because they feel even more helpless than I do. Every day I will set the goal to get through this day and make it the best day I can! Moreover, some days I know my goal will be to just survive and remember that there will be better days.

H is for Hope

Hope no longer means I hope I'll get the job or I hope my party is successful, or I hope I can stay on my diet and fit into my new dress. Hope has taken on new meaning. I hope I survive. I hope I do not suffer too many side effects of treatments. I hope I can keep up my strength. I hope I can continue to hope.

I is for Ignorance

Ignorance frightens me. Ignorance can take so much away from me. Ignorance can scare my friends away from me. Ignorance can take away my courage. I prefer initiative to ignorance because I can take the initiative to seek out the best treatment, to improve my attitude, to accept help and to go on with the fight.

J is for Joy

I must accept every joy in my life more than I ever did before. For now, I appreciate life and its' joys so much more. Now, I can look and see joy in so many little things I took for granted before. Suddenly my priorities have changed and allowed me to see such beauty and joy. Thank you Lord.

K is for Knowledge

I will make myself aware and learn everything I can about a battle I am fighting. I will ask questions. I will read and I will study because knowledge gives me the edge. It fights ignorance and gives strength. Knowledge will make me strong and allow me to help others to be strong. I cannot stop learning. I must be aware.

L is for Love

Love will keep me going. Love will give me the strength and energy I need for my fight. Giving and accepting love will make me stronger. Lord, give me the energy to show my love to my family, friends, doctors, and nurses. Give me the patience to accept love from them. I know that I want to be independent, which sometimes makes it hard to accept the loving help that they need to give.

M is for Memories

Memories of good times past make me happy. They keep fresh as reminders that goals can be attained. Therefore, I relish the memories and make new goals, for that is the only way I can replenish my memories.

N is for NO!

I will not quit! No, I will not stay depressed. No, I will not give in to despair. No, I am not a failure. Yes, I will be successful. Yes, I will survive!

O is for Obstinate

If the cancer can be obstinate, so can I! I will be obstinate when the treatments wear me down, and I will keep positive thoughts even though it is hard. I will try not to be obstinate when my family wants to help. I will let them do what they can because I know it is important for them to help me.

P is for Perseverance

I must persevere. It is a long, hard journey, but the goal at the end is worth it! My blood levels may fall from the drugs that save me, but I will persevere while my blood rebuilds itself. With faith and love, my body will replenish itself.

Q is for Quality

Quality of life is a term commonly used when you are seriously ill. What was my quality of life before I became ill? What is it now? I used to make the decisions. Now it seems as though the disease and the doctors make my decisions for me. Nevertheless, there are some decisions left to me, so I will ask questions and make myself aware of what is happening to me. I cannot make the decision alone but I can work with the doctors in deciding what is best for me. The quality of life for now is that I appreciate everything so much more. I find that little things in life are so much more important.

R is for Rest

I get so tired! I just want to sleep. I must not give in to sleep all the time. I know I need to rest but I must get up and fight! It would be so easy to go to sleep. I cannot give in to the forces of this disease that make me so weak.

S is for Strength

I need strength to fight this disease. I need the strength to make myself look strong because if I look strong, others will treat me as a person with strength and that is what I want to be again, a strong person, free of disease.

T is for Time

God, I wish I had more time! When I am going through treatments, I wish the time would pass more quickly so I could feel good again. I want more time to live, to be with my family, to fulfill my goals. I want more time to say I love you, I am sorry, and thank you. Time….I need more time.

U is for Understanding

I want to ask my family and friends to understand me. Sometimes when I do not feel good, I am short tempered and cross. I do not mean to be. Please understand if my memory is bad. It is hard when you are taking so many medicines. I try to fight it but it is so hard! Please understand I am scared even though I may not say it aloud. I am not even sure I can say the words of cancer, death, or hopeless. They scare me. I try to be positive. Please help me.

V is for Victory

The victory I will attain. I must keep this word foremost in my mind because to be victorious, a soldier must be brave and strong. With the help of my loved ones, and the doctors and nurses, I will be victorious!

W is for Winning

I will win this battle! I will worry at times but I will always come back to a winning attitude because that is how I will survive.

X is for X-rays

Sometimes I think I must glow in the dark after surviving so many x-rays! However, those x-rays are the tools by which my doctors treat my disease. Therefore, I will endure the endless x-rays and leave the album of pictures of my disease at the hospital.

Y is for Yearning

I yearn to be well again! I yearn for my independence, my freedom to do what I want to do, not what the doctor's orders are! However, this yearning will give me the strength to get through this so I will hold it close.

Z is for Zest

I will keep up the battle against this disease until I have zest back in my life!

Love me just a little today
And I will feel ten years younger
Love me just a little today
And I'll feel ten feet taller
Love me just a little today
And the world will seem a better place
Love me just a little today
And the pain of life will be lessened
Love me just a little today
And I will grow and glow
Love me just a little today
And I will love you more.

A month after radiation treatments were completed, Kathy started chemotherapy. We had our consults and made our decision. It was devastating. She had three days of intravenous treatment at the hospital, followed by five days at home, taking 22 pills per day. This went on for months. Her hair, just beginning to grow back, began to fall out again. What did grow back lacked the luster and fullness it had previously had. The area over her right ear remained bald, a result of the massive radiation treatments. We went shopping for wigs and scarves. She took a job in an upscale department store and wanted to look her best. She bought some new clothes and makeup and did everything she could to make herself presentable. She enjoyed working in retail and was looking forward to building a career in it. It was hard though. Monthly chemo left her sick, tired and weak. She never regained a healthy appetite and lost a lot of weight, almost 40 pounds. She had put on some weight in Florida but she was solid from jogging daily. This helped her to survive, though the muscle she had developed quickly deteriorated leaving her weak and frail. Within six months of her surgery, she weighed under a hundred pounds and had little endurance.

Colleen hovered over her, cutting plastic milk bottles to make "puke"buckets for the inevitable nausea and vomiting that accompanied each chemo session. Kathy nicknamed her "Mama Leeny." It was summer break and each day, Colleen made it a point to be home at lunch to fix something for Kathy and encourage her to eat. We endeavored on a campaign to find foods that would be appealing and digestible for her. She lost weight rapidly and by the end of summer, and her 21st birthday, she was extremely thin. Her hair grew back, except for the spot where the intensive radiation had been.

In November we celebrated a "tumor humor party" with the family. We laughed at the illness that had devastated her life. The doctors said that if there was no return of the tumor in six months, it was not likely to come back. We all felt we had beaten it. It felt good to laugh at the monster that had attacked her. We stood together in our fight and won. We cried in joy.

Christmas came, a time of celebration for family. We decorated, as always, and planned to celebrate the day. Working in retail, she was in the heart of the season and enjoying every minute of it. She began to experience momentary lapses at work. When she described what had happened, the description fit what I had read about small seizures. We decided it best to talk to the Oncologist who was on vacation, but available by phone. After we spoke, he called his partner who ordered a CAT scan to be done immediately. Just one month previous, we were so optimistic! The partner called within 24 hours to tell us that there was, in fact, something there again. We could not believe it! We were devastated, to put it mildly. Everything had changed. We were faced with more unanswered questions and the prospect of additional surgery and treatments. The next day, her doctor called to tell us that his new partner had misread the CAT scan. What he saw was the minute amount left after the surgery. There was no tumor growth! I gasped with the news, and immediately felt such anger at the doctor who had made the error. How dare they not verify before telling us! Nevertheless, though it was a scary setback, we were relieved and determined to continue our trek back to normality. We went to Midnight Mass, together as a family, on a very cold Christmas Eve and thanked God for how far we had come.

At the end of the year of chemo, Kathy went to the Oncologist and received the word that there was no more tumor. It was gone! We ran from house to house down the block, announcing our good news to our neighbors. Life, in fact, could begin again for Kathy. After Kathy chided me about my frequent questioning if she was all right, we came to an agreement that if she were not all right, she would tell me. I decided that if she could be that strong, it was time for me to step up to the plate also. Kathy began to take on a new attitude, feeling she had won the battle. She and I attended an Oprah show for cancer survivors. We had beaten it! We were surrounded by positive stories from people who declared they were winners and were now leading productive lives. She started back to work and even began dating. Years later, I found her journal, tucked away on a closet shelf where she related the demoralizing effects of wearing the wig. She wrote about enjoying a date and when her date kissed her goodnight, he would realize she was wearing a wig, and that was the last she would hear of him. She was confident that when the right person came along, it would not matter, but finding someone like that was not easy. It was hard because friends were away at school and though she was gregarious, making new friends took time and no one understood the effects of a brain tumor. When people do not understand, they withdraw and avoid.

Three years after Kathy's surgery, she was holding her own. It was rough, but she was hanging in there. Our lives had changed forever, yet we strove to act as if nothing had changed. Schedules were different for every one. Colleen was finishing high school. Kathy worked and was looking at taking some classes at the Junior College. Patrick was working and going to school. Somehow, the hectic pace we were keeping eased us into a lifestyle that was normal, at least to our standards. Day-to-day problems are always there, but after a serious illness, the simple tasks of going to work and school become a joy that you look forward to.

Colleen worked late every night on her Senior Orchesis Dance show at the high school. Kathy and I loved to go early and watch her energy on stage every chance we had. For a few moments we could mentally feel the freedom and grace of movement. Since that breathless gasp back in the hotel room, I had literally been holding my breath, sporadically allowing just enough air in for survival. Watching Colleen on stage gave me a feeling of release, a momentary escape from the daily fears I was facing. She was rehearsing every night and one of us would pick her up to hear the updates and the joy in her experiences. It was an exhausting but happy time. One night, as the time approached to pick her up, the phone, which I had begun to fear, rang. "Please come, Colleen is very upset." Kathy and I raced to the school to find Colleen devoured in a cloud of dancers, hovering over her, as she cried and cried and cried. When I got to her, she just said, "It was like it was happening all over again". The day Kathy suffered the seizure; Colleen had reacted admirably. I knew that day as I looked at Colleen sitting on the edge of the bed, her face as white as the sheets she sat on, that this memory would never leave her. Pat went in the ambulance with Kathy and I stayed back with Colleen to sooth her and get dressed to go to the hospital. She did not cry, then, or for three years. Until that night at rehearsal when a classmate started hyperventilating and the teacher called the paramedics. When they arrived, Colleen was instantly taken back to that moment in the hotel room. Just a few weeks after the show, Colleen graduated high school. Our youngest bird was fleeing the nest. She was enrolled in college for the fall, where she would major in dance. As we celebrated her graduation, we felt our family had survived the worst and now was going on to better times. There was nothing we could not do together.

Love and marriage
Family and kids
Growing old together
You and I
Hopes and dreams fulfilled
We'll walk the moonlit beaches
Hand in hand
The twilight years will be good
Just you and I
The years have passed so quickly
Honeymoon into childbirth
One, two, surprise! There's a third
Diapers, fevers, scrapes, and scratches
Now I learn my ABC's
Girl Scouts, Boy Scouts, baseball, and dance
Science fairs, recitals, field trips and parties
A movie out, just you and me, would be nice.
A night alone, remember what that was like?
Learning how to drive, prom night and college
Twenty-five years have passed. Where did they go?
Driving, cooking, cleaning, teaching, working and shopping
Three kids in three different schools. Which PTA meeting is tonight?
First communion, Confirmation, rush from one to the other
Graduation, look how big she's gotten!
Twenty-five years, our Silver Anniversary
Now it is our time, time for us, for you and me
Tropical breezes are calling.
A moonlight cruise would be nice
We will wine and we will dine, together
BANG! There goes that dream of you and me together
Fate has struck again and we must adjust
Thank God you are alive
Now we will rewrite the script for just you and I

Our twenty-fifth anniversary was approaching. With our three kids standing by us, we renewed our wedding vows in front of family and friends. One thing was left before Pat and I could really celebrate our completion of 25 years of marriage. The kids had all graduated high school and were either in college or working. We could now talk about a weekend together, a cruise, a vacation, just the two of us. Colleen's last recital was the only thing left. She begged me to help backstage. Pat said I really did not need to. Nevertheless, I thought this was the last time I could do this for her. I could not know that there would be no plans for Pat and I, or that our lives were about to drastically change again. Sunday night I came home from the recital, breathing a sigh of relief that it was over. Pat had caught a cold. He was coughing. He went to bed early to try to shake it off. The next day I had to work late and when I arrived home, his cough was worse. I ran to the pharmacy and got some cough medicine. The next morning, he came to kiss me goodbye and brought me a cup of coffee. I asked him if he felt better and he agreed that the new cough medicine had helped. It was a usual morning, a usual good-bye. He said he would call me at 11:30, which he always did. There was a peace within me that we had successfully raised our three kids and now could enter into a new phase in our lives. With both of us working, finances were no longer a problem. We had survived, together. I enjoyed my cup of coffee and got ready for work. He had been gone about an hour. As I pulled into the parking lot, my boss was standing in the drive, waiting for me. My thoughts were as to why he would be so impatient since I had worked until seven the night before. As I got out of my car, he told me that Colleen had called and Pat was in the emergency room. The hospital was just next door to where I worked, but he offered to drive me and stayed in case I needed support. We arrived at the emergency room, my heart pounding. What could have happened? I saw Pat… He was sitting up, alert, and complaining. The doctor came to see us, "There is a subachronoid bleed. We will be taking him to intensive care." All right, what is a subachronoid bleed? What is a subachronoid? They put me to work on admitting papers and then sent me to intensive care. Colleen, Kathy and my mom had arrived. I went in and found Pat in a dark, quiet corner, heavily sedated. The doctor approached me and took me to the desk. "I want you to bring someone in with you and I will explain everything to both of you." I went out and the girls decided Colleen should be the one. We returned to the unit and sat with the doctor, who drew pictures describing the artery in Pat's brain that had an opening the size of a pin and was bleeding into his brain. We were warned not to attempt to wake him. We must be very quiet and not cause any noise that could startle him. If we did, there was a danger the bleed could become worse and he could die instantly. He went on to tell us of the surgery he planned to do and the hoped for results. Within hours, he was in surgery to correct the bleed and insert a shunt to avoid fluid accumulation on the brain, a common complication of this surgery. I remember being enveloped in the soft white leather couches in the hospital lobby as we waited for Pat to come out of surgery. I had succumbed to an exhaustive sleep when I felt a pen tickle my arm. I opened my eyes to the smiling face of the surgeon, who said everything had gone well and Pat was in recovery. Again, there should be no disturbances. By the next morning, he was awake, hungry, and arguing with nurses. The doctor came in and said, "This man does not need to be in intensive care. Transfer him to a room on the surgical floor." It was safe to breathe again. We had survived again. As I went home that evening to rest, I was stunned, thinking, two brain surgeries in one family! It just could not be, but it was. I stayed with him all of Saturday as the kids and family called and came to visit. He was getting irritable, wanting to get out of bed. He kept joking about the surgical staples in his head. I kissed him goodnight and went home to sleep. Everything was going to be okay. We beat the odds again.

Visiting hours did not begin until noon on Sunday. I went to church where the congregation prayed for Pat. I picked up a Sunday newspaper and went to the hospital to spend a quiet afternoon with him. I knew something was wrong when I entered the room. His head was swollen and he was incoherent. The nurses carefully avoided my questions until the doctor came. "There's been a complication. Microsurgery irritates the brain, which is a muscle, and causes spasms. These spasms cause the arteries to pinch off the blood supply." It all sounded so sophisticated. He was suffering a stroke and there was nothing they could do to stop it. I remember standing in the door of Pat's room and listening while the doctor instructed the nurses on his care. "I need you to understand and do exactly what I tell you." It sounded so desperate.

By that night, he was not communicating at all. They took him down for a CAT scan and I was beginning to wonder if I was going to find myself a widow, after surviving so much. I stayed the night, because frankly, I do not think they expected him to last the night. The next day, the damage reports were in. Left side paralysis, and severe left neglect, which meant his brain was not registering anything on his left side. Since I worked so close to the hospital, I went to help him eat lunch, and returned for dinner. The kids pitched in to care for the house, assuring me they would handle everything, and admonished me not to worry. My hands were full, learning how bad it was for Pat and what our future would be like. We found he could not walk nor use his left arm. He ate only the food on the right side of his plate, unless you turned the plate full circle to expose the remaining food to his now limited visual field. When the rehab doctor came to evaluate him, we found he had lost the ability to add, subtract, multiply, and divide. Later, in rehab, a nun friend of ours came to visit, and he said, "Sister, I forgot all of my tables." After one month in the hospital, he was transferred to the rehab center where he would stay for two more months and go into outpatient rehab for another six months. I began to wonder if we could beat this one. We went to family support meetings. I learned how to help him transfer from the wheelchair to bed, toilet, car, etc. He learned how to dress, toilet and eat, with one arm. He had vision therapy to force himself to look to the left to get the whole picture. They described his visual loss like walking into a room full of people, but only seeing the people in the middle, unaware that there were more on the sides. I prayed, I cried, I read. I studied how the brain works and what the effects of stroke and disability are. I fought the therapists when they said I was in denial. I remember the first day I took him to the rehab. They took him in with a group of men who were playing wheelchair ball. They were swiveling their chairs to punch, kick, and toss at a bright red ball. Pat could not even track the ball. The social worker took me into her office and sat me by a bright sunny window, where I proceeded to cry my eyes out. My firstborn child, and now my husband. Why God? Why? After I emptied a box of Kleenex, I will never forget this woman who coldly looked at me and said, "You will survive this." My mouth dropped open as I thought, "you cold hearted bitch." I did survive.

As rehab moved on, we had passes for the day to go to a restaurant, go home for a meal or take a ride. I did not know why handicap parking spaces took up two spaces until I had to unload a wheelchair and transfer my husband from car to chair. This was no small feat, but one that had to be accomplished. This was all in preparation for bringing a wheelchair bound patient home and how to care for him. I had no clue how our lives would change. I desperately wanted to make things normal again. I remember stopping at the supermarket late at night, after leaving rehab. I stood in line behind a couple our age, holding hands, chatting, enjoying each other. I felt so cheated! I realized that we would never walk on that beach hand in hand. Going to the beach now meant parking his wheelchair on the walk at the edge of the sand, and walking the surf, alone. The reality assaulted me that Pat would not return to work. His work people began to visit, obviously trying to find out how bad he was. They agreed to let him return to work, if he could drive. He said there was no problem. Three weeks and three accidents later, I took the keys and said, "No way." That took his life away. His job, his freedom, his independence were now all gone. Now I was the major breadwinner. I was the head of the household. No moonlit beaches for us. Life was now taking care of Pat and working as many hours as I could because we needed the money.

The family we had been, the couple who had it all, was no more. We were broken, too broken to fix. Kathy's hair would not grow back. Wearing a wig was a way of life for her. She would remain thin and weak, no matter how she desired to be strong. Pat would never be whole again. His vision would not return. His brain would not function as before. He would remain paralyzed on the left side, and we would never stroll down that moonlit beach together. Life, as we knew it, as we planned it, would never be the same. I so wanted us to succeed, in some way. I was buoyed with stories of success. Wheelchair patients who learned how to play basketball in their wheelchairs. Blind people who scaled mountains. Story after story of people who overcame adversity. I acquired an obsession for self-help books and shows. We would overcome!

I sat to watch our new cable television one evening, surfing the channels to find something inspiring. I stopped on a religious channel and listened as they prayed. They went on to give their messages from God as they looked into the camera. Suddenly, I heard the man say, "There is a girl with something in her head, on the right side, I'm not sure, but it's going to be okay, God is with you." God had spoken. He had sent me a message. We would survive. A few weeks later, I stopped at home for lunch. As I surfed up and down the list, I stopped at another religious channel where another minister was praying. I thought perhaps I would receive another message of encouragement, and stopped to hear the word of God. Instead, the words loudly came from the television, "You there, you who are switching channels up and down, stop!" Another message from God? I turned off the TV and returned to work. I have always been a prayerful person. I do not feel I could survive a day without my faith in God. I have always had a special closeness to the Blessed Virgin who has answered many of my needs. I fervently prayed the rosary those days, establishing a constant contact with heaven to help me through all my challenging days. It was all I could do to get through each day. Our routine became one of getting Pat ready for pickup to go to rehab and then leaving for work. I had some wonderful neighbors to greet Pat when he came home on the days when Colleen could not get home from school on time. Kathy was away at school by then and Patrick was working and going to school. Church groups and friends called to offer help, but because of the tunnel vision, mental confusion frustrated Pat when strangers or too many people came by. We existed, but money was tight, very tight. We still had hopes that Pat would return to some kind of job. When I got home in the evening, I fixed dinner, cleaned house and helped Pat get ready for bed. I would collapse late at night and fall asleep in front of the TV, many times waiting for Colleen to return from her commute to school. My job became increasingly demanding. I was one of those women who had learned to work harder and harder and if everything was not done, it was my fault. I was exhausted! I remember collapsing in a lump on the bathroom floor as I was helping Pat out of the shower one evening, begging him to try to help. Colleen calling out to me in a voice that I knew meant something was wrong interrupted my mini breakdown. I ran out to the hall to see Colleen with a bleeding face, puffy eye, crying. I thought she had been mugged or raped in the parking lot at school! I calmed her and placed an ice pack on her eye before running back to help Pat finish his preparations for bed. I could not share with him, because his mental capabilities were just not there yet. As soon as he was tucked in, I went back to Colleen, who related how she was working alone in the dance studio at school (she was a dance major), working on completing a complex flip. She flipped the wrong way, fell flat on her face, breaking her nose, blackening her eye, suffering some small facial cuts, and broke her finger. We continued to ice her eye, nose and hand before she finally fell into bed. The next day, I had already arranged to take off to take Pat to the eye doctor to determine what his visual capabilities would be. At this time he was still in the wheelchair. The next

HAS ANYONE SEEN MY DAISY?

day Colleen with her bruises, and I, helped Pat into the car, storing the wheelchair in back, and left a little early to go to the ear, nose, and throat specialist to see what damage she had done. As she sat in the patient chair with all of her bruises, and Pat sat in the wheelchair, still looking pretty beat up, with his arm in a sling and scars from his surgery, the doctor entered, took one look, turned to me, and said, "What I want to know is what happened to the other guy?" We all burst out laughing, which we had begun to find out was the only type of healing available to us.

From there we went to the orthopedic doctor where Colleen's finger was set and then on to the eye doctor to find that Pat's tunnel vision was worse than we thought, and would never get better. They said it was the worst case of left neglect they had ever seen. The next day I returned to work to a boss who was getting increasingly impatient with my needs to take off so many days. Accidents happen to everyone. When our kids were young, we had our share of scrapes and bruises and trips to the emergency room for shots and stitches. Nevertheless, when serious illness strikes, minor incidents just become one more thing in a line of occurrences. As they pile up, everyone around you, as well as you, take on the pattern of thinking, "what's next." It puts you in a habit of negative thinking, which leads to bitterness. If you succumb to this, you will be bitter and the negatives will overcome the positives. Joking and laughing at ourselves was our way keeping the bitterness at bay. If you do not hang on to that glass half full thinking, bitterness is all there is. I could not accept that.

One + one is two, 2 + 2 is 4, or so they say
First grade, second grade, addition, subtraction
Third grade, fourth grade, multiplication and division
Fifth grade, sixth grade, learn those tables
Seventh grade, eighth grade, algebra comes along
One moment, one accident, and all is gone
Learn them again, study very hard
2x4 = ?????
It just isn't there....

The scariest moment in my life was hearing the rehab doctor questioning Pat. I knew that there was significant damage in the visual area. For a month, I had been coming into his room, calling "hi" as I entered from the left side of the room. He would always look to the right, seeking me out, only realizing where I was as I walked around to his right. So many times, as I entered and his food tray was still in front of him, I would ask if he was going to finish. His response was always, "Look mom, I finished it all," until I turned the plate around and showed him the other half. His mind was only seeing the right half. The food was sectioned exactly down the middle as if he had drawn a line with a ruler down the center of the plate. However, the night the doctor was questioning him, I realized the severity of the brain damage. "How much is 2+2?" No answer. "How much is 7 + 5?" No answer. The questions went on and the answers remained elusive, clearly showing the extent of what his mental disability would be. It was determined to transfer him to rehab within the week. The plan was to get a brace for his left leg, a sling for his left arm, get him walking, do occupational therapy to teach him how to live with his disability, i.e. bathing, eating, dressing, etc. Nothing was planned for his loss of cognitive abilities, or how (or if) he would be able to return to work. When he was released from inpatient rehab, we had three days of testing to determine what his capabilities would be to return to the workforce. Math was still nonexistent. He tried to balance our checkbook, and quickly showed the disaster that would be. If the amount was $20.00, it became $20,000. We live in a mathematical world. You have to be able to do at least simple math just to exist in the work world. I was not ready to give up. I had hopes (they said denial) that his left neglect would improve. I prayed daily for a miracle. When they were ready to release him from outpatient rehab, I borrowed money to take him on a weekend trip to Disneyworld. He was depressed, remembering all the camping trips we had made there, and realizing that it would never be the same. I hoped that the weekend would let him know that his life was not over and that there were things we could do. He was still dependent on the wheelchair so it was an exhausting trip for me. However, on the airplane, I began to figure. We talked about the future and I said, "No one is going to take care of us, we must do it ourselves."I figured that we had both run other people's businesses, why couldn"t we do it ourselves. I set out a plan.

First things first, I found a program at our local junior college for brain injured adults, where they were taught mathematical functions and skills previously learned in grade school. Pat attended classes for 8 weeks and amazingly regained the majority of his math skills, though the $20/$20,000 problem remained. What the heck, I would balance the checkbook.

A good day's work is rewarding.
A good paycheck at the end of the week is delightful.
Reputation, experience, skills, and the will to perform.
Ah, we teach it to our children.
But life has changed.
A good job done is not enough.
A gold watch at the end of your term is not promised
Job security, increased pay, insurance and benefits
We take it all for granted.
I'm down, I'm out, and now I will start over.

After about a year of apologizing for time needed to take Pat to the doctor, and receiving an excellent annual review, with a mere 4% raise, it was clear that I must be looking at another way. I started a maid service and hired one employee. I picked her up in the morning, dropped her at the first house, and went on to start my workday. At lunch, I picked her up and dropped her at the next house for the afternoon. I then returned to work, completed my tasks, picking her up on my way home, and after dropping her at her house, returned to my home to fix dinner, do laundry, etc, etc. Within six months, my business had grown significantly enough to leave my job. Within four months of leaving my job, I had over 12 employees and the business income had increased over seven times. I felt powerful. I knew I could do it. I was quickly approached about franchising, but did not have the money to finance it. When I told Patrick I was starting my own business, he questioned what I knew about running my own business. My quick response was that I really did not know, but I was willing to find out. I did. I learned to give quotes on jobs, figure salaries, do payroll, hire, and fire. I hired one of Pat's retired friends to drive the van to take our workers to and from jobs and the train. We had our first official Christmas party at

MacDonald's with Pat, Kathy (who had started working for us in the office) and me. Was there a chance that we would overcome and come out together and happy again?

I had carefully figured out what our assets were, and they were shrinking fast. I looked at my ability to support us and the promises were not great. I had always been a secretary, working my way up to office manager, administrative assistant, and eventually district administrator for a large computer firm. The title meant nothing. When I asked our new Regional Manager for a raise because of the extra duties I was taking on, he stated that I did not need a raise because "You have a husband who works." That's the way things were. That was when I left to find better things. Pat's stroke occurred just six weeks into my new employment. When he was in the hospital, I worked so hard, arriving at 6:30am instead of 8:00am, so I could go to the hospital at lunch, return to work, and leave by 5:00pm to back to help Pat with dinner. It was clear that Pat would not be able to return to a thriving position. Because of his tunnel vision, he could not drive, though we even tried a second go around at therapy to teach him to accommodate it. There was no doubt that if we were to make it, it would be up to me. We gathered the family together one Sunday afternoon to let them know that I was going to start my own business, and that we hoped it would be tremendously successful. Kathy was not doing too well at her retail job and was frequently exhausted. We asked her to come to work for us, running the office with Pat, so I could be in the field. We were quite a team! Beat up, battered, still together and doing a hell of a job!

I Am Woman
As the song says, "No one's ever going to beat me down again"
A woman's place is in the home
A woman's place is behind her husband
A woman's place is to be kept, two steps behind her man
What happens when…?
The man is not there….
What happens when…?
The man cannot do the job….
What happens when…?
The roles are reversed…
What happens then?

I was nineteen years old when we married. I was shy, quiet, and afraid of everything. My "man" was going to take care of me. HE would succeed. HE would make lots of money. HE would lead the family. HE would take care of me. Now the fact was that there would be no active retirement life for us. There would be no walks on moonlit beaches, holding hands and breathing in the air of a successful and fulfilled life together. I would forever be destined to walking a little behind him. Since his peripheral vision was gone, he was unaware of my presence beside him. His concentration was forward and attacking each step as if it were a hill to be climbed. His left arm hangs in a sling and his right hand holds his cane. His eyes are focused ahead, the picture frame of life erased forever. Pat was one of many who said, "I don't need disability insurance, I have life insurance." Disability insurance premiums were very high. The question was never posed as to what would happen if you did not die. Though he worked for a large builder/developer at the time of his stroke, they were now clearly on a path of getting rid of him. He was a liability. They placed him in dangerous situations, insisting that if he could not handle it, he could not have the job. Of course he couldn't handle it, and they eventually coerced him into resigning, benevolently offering us COBRA insurance. We found out later that there was no benevolence involved. It was the law! It was new law and we were not aware of it at the time that everything occurred. They did not want to take responsibility for him on the job. Rights for the disabled had not yet been won. I, on the other hand, woke up to what the world was really like. I could depend only on me. I set about learning everything I could about business, payroll, management, and business finances. I was fierce in my dedication to succeed and enduring in maintaining my tasks as wife, mother, and daughter to my aging mother. I switched my hats from hour to hour when necessary. I worked no less than sixty hours per week. I drifted into sleep reading self-improvement and positive thinking books and articles. There was nothing that could stop me. My family would survive and come out ahead! It was up to me, and me alone, to make this happen.

For three years we went on like this. My business grew 600% in the first full year of business. I followed the theory of the five-year plan. The first year was based on, "I'm a nice person; you should do business with me." By the second year, people should be saying, "I've heard of your company." By the third year, you should be breaking even and by the fifth year, making a profit. It was a labor-intensive business and labor costs were high. What I finally brought home was not enough. I was hoping to turn that corner and start reaping a profit. Nowhere in the plan was there room for disaster to strike again.

Here Comes the Bride
The bride comes down the aisle
All faces turned to her
Her beauty shines
Her happiness abounds
The future is hopeful
The present is a joy
Nothing can hold back
The tears of joy she cries
Joy, joy, here comes the bride

After a tumultuous period of adjustment, Kathy met the man who was to be her husband. They seemed very much in love. Kathy was happy, and that was what counted to us. They met in November and were engaged on Valentine's Day, with the wedding planned for August. Brightness filled the house again as plans for the wedding began. Rent the hall, find the dresses, plan the showers, and send the invitations. Even though I was working as hard as ever, happiness was settling in. Hope for the future was again present. Fear was pushed back. Kathy had won the battle.

She was still very thin and weak, but made a beautiful bride. Everyone said she looked like a Dresden doll. She was so easy to work with in planning the wedding. She was so happy to be getting married, to be like everyone else, she would just say, "Whatever you want, Mom". When duplicate gifts arrived, she said,"It's not polite to return gifts; we'll find use for them as time goes on."She did not fight, complain, or insist on anything. I almost felt bad that she was not taking more control of her wedding, but her generous attitude made me want to do more for her.

That summer was one of the hottest in history with an over abundance of 90 degree, plus days. We were so concerned that she would faint on her very special day. However, the day before the wedding, a cool front whispered in, with no thunderstorms to announce it, just a cool, fragrant, summer breeze. The day was fantastic. I remembered standing at the foot of her hospital bed the day the doctor called and in fierce determination, promised, "I'll dance at your wedding!" I did! We danced, laughed, and had a wonderful time. Many came back to our house after the reception and continued to celebrate. It was so normal! It felt so good!

A Child is born
A grandchild to spoil!
Or so they say
Grandparents must keep their place
It's now up to mom and dad.
Grandparents can enjoy special moments
And then go home
Grandparents can go on to other things,
Career, hobbies, and new friends, ones that you did not meet through PTA.
My daughter, my first born, is pregnant.
They never thought she could
But yep, she is, and oh so happy
Tears of joy streamed down her face
"I'm pregnant mom"
What precious words to hear!
Planning for months ahead. Showers and gifts
It is a time of celebration, a time of joy for all
BANG! Change of plans I'm afraid
Early arrival by 3 months, the minuscule babe is born
On life support, under bright lights, he lay in his plastic womb
Tiniest of fingers and toes, not even able to suck
All together though, except no eyelashes!
He is a person born to this world
"He's Kevin Paul," she affirmed
And he was named

Kathy had been coming in late, or calling in sick, complaining of nausea. After a few weeks, I asked, "Kathy, do you think you're pregnant"? "No, no way, Mom.". A week later, I asked again and said, "Maybe you ought to see your doctor."She made the appointment and called me in tears. "Mom, I am pregnant!"The doctors never thought she could get pregnant, not in a million years. She had maximum radiation and one year of chemotherapy. Surely, she was no longer fertile. They were wrong. She began to feel better and got a little tummy on her. Her genuine smile relayed the happiness she felt. She was finally "normal,"just like any other young girl, married a year and a half, and now pregnant.

That Christmas, when she was just six months, we included new baby gifts in anticipation of the child who would be with us next Christmas.

She had been so thin since her surgery and treatments; we teased her about her growing belly. She continued to work in the office with all the employees congratulating her on her pregnancy.

In January, she began to spot, and went to the doctor. They put her in the hospital and quickly became concerned about her increasing blood pressure. Within the week, they transferred her to a hospital that specialized in premature births. They monitored her carefully, trying to give the baby every chance of survival. On visits, we would listen to the baby's heartbeat, with ever-increasing anticipation of our first grandchild. After about a week, her blood pressure began to climb higher and they could not bring it down. They warned that they might need to do a C-section soon. They began to administer steroids to help the baby's lungs. On January 22, 1990, they called and said they were taking her into surgery, no more waiting. The baby might not survive. For that matter, we could lose her also. As we dashed to the hospital, I prayed that if there were any justice in this world, Kathy and that baby will survive. She was already in surgery when we got there. We sat anxiously waiting for news. As the elevator doors opened, the doctor came out with a huge grin and said, "She's fine, and she has a little boy!" He then went on to tell us that the baby only weighed 2lbs. 9ozs and would be in the neonatal intensive care unit. We greeted Kathy as she was rolled by on a gurney to her room. She was so happy! She was tired but happy. She firmly announced that the baby's name would be Kevin Paul, and we all sighed. Kathy had survived again, and now had her little baby boy. We went to the nursery and looked in awe at the tiny baby, with 10 fingers and 10 toes, a wrinkly little face, everything in tact, except no eyebrows or eyelashes. He was in an incubator with a tube in his nose. He was just 26 weeks in gestation! What a miracle! If anyone thought that late term abortion was okay, they needed to look at this baby, tiny as he was, fully developed, and breathing on his own. His general health was determined to be good. He had not yet learned the sucking instinct so they needed to teach him. He had a six inch "Winnie the Pooh" toy in his incubator and it was bigger than he was! Kathy was released a few days later, but Kevin stayed another six weeks in the hospital. Nightly, she would go to him, feed him, diaper him, and hold him. She was serene. She was so happy, anticipating the day she could bring him home.

Life begins against all odds
Kevin Paul did grow, he did
For two months he laid in his plastic womb
With mom there to hold him for just a few minutes a day
Her love and joy wrapped around him
As she swaddled him in her arms
The joy in her face brightened his tiny body
Her hopes of a normal life enlightened
Illness, treatments, now behind her
Life is good and she would enjoy
BANG! Change of plans
The tumor has returned. We must operate.
Treatments? No. There are no more.
Life, happiness, hope, goes into cold storage
Survival, miracles, and faith are the topics of the day
She will survive!
By all that is right and holy, God will save her!
Won't He?

March 16, 1990 was the day for Kevin to be released to the world. Kathy and baby came by our house for the afternoon while her husband returned to work. Kevin weighed a whopping four and a half pounds at his release! It was Friday and they were looking forward to the weekend to adjust to life with a baby in the house. Kathy fed and diapered the baby all afternoon, smiling with the pleasure of new motherhood. Her husband picked them up that evening and there was a feeling of peace and hope as they left. Life was indeed returning to normal. I am woman….I had kept everything together and now we were being rewarded with the blessings of new life.

Saturday was their day. We did not know it would be the only day of normalcy they would ever have, a couple adjusting to life with a new baby in the house. Sunday, they came for brunch so the rest of the family could hold the baby. Intensive care nurseries only allow the parents and occasionally grandparents to enter and hold the child. The rest of the family could only stand on the other side of the glass and observe the baby. As my family gathered for a happy occasion, life seemed normal again. I felt a twinge of worry as Kathy complained of dizziness when she got up from the dinner table. I suggested she might call the doctor and check on her medication levels because they had taken her off anti-seizure medications while she was pregnant and there was a definite possibility that the levels could be off. As they left that afternoon, I looked at Pat with concern. "Don't worry so much. It will be fine. She just needs to get her meds checked." The plan was for her husband to drop her off the next morning so we could help her with the baby.

The next morning her husband called from work and asked me to go to their apartment and pick Kathy and the baby up. He complained that he could not get her up. I was at a very important meeting and never anticipating the worst, I said I would be there as soon as I could. I could not comprehend that he had left her alone with a premature baby who needed constant care while she was not responsive. I arrived about 10:30am. Kathy was in bed with the baby, who was crying fiercely. I asked if she had fed him. She said her husband had fed him before he left, just a short time ago. It had, in fact, been three hours ago. Kevin needed to eat every two hours because he was still so small. I gently took the baby and changed his drenched diaper, urging Kathy to get dressed. I got the baby clean, fed, and began to pack up the necessities to go to our house. Kathy was having problems with dizziness and walking and I was gaining concern. When we got to our house, she fell asleep for a few hours. When she awoke, I helped her feed the baby. She was happy, but just not herself. After dinner, as they left, I urged her husband to call the neurologist regarding her medications, feeling strongly that she needed to have the levels checked. One of the signs of toxicity from one med was a drunk-like state with dizziness, disorientation, and altered gait. I was confident this was the problem, but could not impress on my son-in-law the importance of reaching the doctor. This was only the beginning of communication problems with my son-in-law. He clearly did not see the importance of my request and chose to walk away from it. Legally, I could not call the doctor myself. They were both adults and were the only ones with power to speak to the doctor. Kathy was functioning poorly and needed someone to speak for her. As she was married, I could not do that. Attempts to help him understand the urgency were futile.

HAS ANYONE SEEN MY DAISY?

The next day when I went to pick her up, I suggested we stop by the hospital and asked to see her neurosurgeon. She agreed and was eager to show him her baby. He came and smiled at the baby and observed Kathy. He said perhaps we should do a blood test. He expressed no concern, so I thought we were still okay. Get the medications adjusted and all would be well. I took Kathy and the baby back to our house where she again fell asleep for several hours, waking to sit and feed the baby. I was busy with work, so we arranged for the next day that her husband would drop the baby by us and Kathy would remain home by herself to rest, which we hoped would help. He picked up the baby on his way home. I called to see how Kathy was doing and he thought that perhaps she had fallen during the day. She was bruised. He was not sure. I again urged him to contact the doctor. The next morning, I called my mother after he dropped the baby off and asked her to go to Kathy's and stay with her. She hurried over and did the wash, cooked and cleaned and generally looked out for Kathy, who was mainly sleeping.

On Friday morning, which was my company payroll day, her husband called and said he had to go to work and again could not get Kathy up. I was giving up on trying to help him understand. If he was willing to walk out and leave the baby even though he knew Kathy was not able to care for herself, let alone the baby, I did not know how to convince him. I called my mother and told her to meet me over at their apartment, hoping that with her help, we could get through the day. When we arrived, I had to let us in with the spare key they had given me. The baby was sleeping. We could not get Kathy out of bed. Every time she attempted to sit up, the dizziness overwhelmed her. I tried to reach her husband but he was not answering. My mom and I both tried to get Kathy up but she could not walk across the hall to the bathroom, even with our help. I decided I had to call the paramedics and get her to the hospital, still assuming her medications were causing her problems. They took her away in the ambulance. My mother and I returned to our house with the baby and I left her and Pat to handle things there. I returned to the hospital, full of questions. She was in the ER. Her husband had not come. I sat by her side, assuring her everything would be fine. After eight hours, and no husband, the doctor came to me and asked where her husband was. I admitted I could not understand why he was not there. The doctor took me to a little room off the ER. I remember thinking, that it must be pretty bad when they take you into a little room. It was. The tumor had returned worse than before. She would be transferred to intensive care immediately. Yes, I knew where it was, and what to do. Been there, done that, sorry to say. After her husband finally got there, I went home to break the news to the family. Here we were again. Saturday, I had to deliver the overdue paychecks to our employees, giving them the news. It was usually Kathy who gave out paychecks. They all warmly greeted me and expressed their concern for Kathy. They told me not to worry. They would handle everything. The rest of Saturday was spent scheduling shifts to care for the baby and visiting Kathy at the intermittent intensive care visiting hours.

Sunday we went to church and prayed. Please God, not again. Sunday afternoon, as we were preparing to leave for the hospital, the neurosurgeon called. He had not been able to find her husband to speak with him. He was visiting with the baby at his parents' home and had not even called the hospital to check on his wife. "I just want someone to know that your daughter has a one in one hundred chance of surviving three days."That damn phone again! I thought I would never answer a phone again. In fact, it took me several years to get over the fear of the phone ringing and what bad news it was to announce. I still cringe if the phone rings, or one of my kids calls and tentatively say the word Mom. My heart always skips a beat, anticipating bad news. A couple of years later, our son, Patrick, called and asked to come over, that he had something to tell us. I nervously counted the minutes in anticipation of what terrible thing had attacked him. I kept busy trying not to worry. When he came, we sat down at the dining room table, and he told us he was leaving his wife of seven years, and asked if he could stay with us for a couple of weeks. My reaction? "My God, Patrick, I thought you were going to tell us you were suffering from a brain tumor or something that bad. I'm sorry to hear about your marriage, but I'm sure things will work out."When you go through all of this, your priorities become skewed. Let's see, what's worse, a malignant brain tumor or a couple splitting up. I did not want either, but I knew that a break up could be talked about and both parties could come to a mutual agreement. They had been together long enough, I had faith they could work things out. Sad, but true. However, a brain tumor or a stroke? That is permanent. Your life changes and nothing can make it right again. I knew that all too well.

After the doctor's call, we rushed to the hospital that night to be with Kathy. They said she was now paralyzed on the right side. From Sunday afternoon to Monday night, we prayed, we hovered, and we called friends and family. People came to pray with us. People laid their hands on her. The news was consuming us…could she really die? I recalled that day when the doctor had called and told me "There's something there," I had gone to the hospital and stood at the foot of her bed and prayed, "Please God, at least allow her to live long enough to know the love of a man, marry and have a child, the dreams most young girls have." Seven and a half years later, I stood at the foot of her bed again and said, "God, I didn't mean literally!" The doctor ordered all but one of us to go home and get some rest. It was agreed that her husband should be with her. The doctors were trying a new course of treatment and by noon on Tuesday, she would be greatly improved or she would be gone. How do you deal with that? I felt like I had been leading my life facing death! I prayed again, "If there is a just God, she will survive!" When we arrived the next morning, she was indeed more alert. The doctor gathered us together to tell us we had a new option, surgery. The tumor had in fact grown back, but instead of being on the peripheral of the brain, it was growing down towards the hypothalamus. She was paralyzed on the right side. They could remove some of the tumor to relieve the pressure, but it was not a cure, we were just buying time. We said we would take it!

Kathy asked for a day with the family and wanted to have the baby baptized. Her husband arranged for a priest to come to the hospital the following day. We brought a hastily dressed baby in the family baptismal outfit and laid him on her chest. At that point, she could not even move her head. Colleen raced back from school to be there and Pat and I were now Godparents, as well as grandparents, to Kevin. As Kathy's eyes darted towards the baby, the priest did his blessings and Kevin Paul was baptized. We took the baby home, leaving Kathy, and her husband to contemplate the next day's surgery. I firmly believe that God answers our prayers. I had been told to be specific in my prayers. That day in May in 1983, I was specific: at least long enough to get married and have a child. My prayers were answered, exactly. The surgery went smoothly and we greeted Kathy in Intensive Care. Her right side appeared to be still paralyzed, but it was too early to tell. Although the immediacy had slowed down, the problem was not gone. The doctor had told us, "We're just buying time." As soon as possible, they moved Kathy to a regular room, a large one, with no roommate, so we could bring the baby to her. Late on the first night in that room, as she lay alone, she felt the urge to urinate. She pressed the buzzer, and no one answered. She pressed it again and again, but to no avail. She really had to go and the idea of not being able to walk to the bathroom filled her with frustration. As she continued to wait for help, she became more and more determined to overcome this new disability. She dropped herself out of bed, crawled to the bathroom to use the toilet, and crawled back to bed. However, as she got to the bed, she felt a renewed strength in her right side and she stood. Was it a miracle? I do not know. At that point, we needed many miracles and acceptance of this regained independence was enough to be thankful for at this point.

Within days, she came home and was able to feed and cuddle with the baby. Her right side was still weak, but we helped her get situated and placed the baby in her arms. I have read that there is a theory that there is a hormonal bond between mother and newborn and that it continues for almost a year, while that special mother/child bond is formed. If that theory is correct, she at least had the opportunity to give Kevin the benefit of a mother's love, and for that, I shall be forever thankful. As we attempted to get back into a routine, we relaxed into pseudo happiness, enjoying Kathy's renewed energy and the daily joys of a new baby. By the second week, as reality began to sink in, I had increasing concerns about what would be next. Her husband could not function well enough to anticipate what the near future might hold, so it was up to us to foresee that we needed a plan. I went to Pat who also had settled into a false complacency of the day-to-day life with a houseful of family. We had Kathy, her husband, and the baby, our son, who was getting ready to move out, our younger daughter, my mother, and a dog!

I asked Pat why he was not as inquisitive as he had been the first time around. He agreed that we must do something, took out his old list of contacts, and began to make calls to various doctors and the Brain Tumor Research Association in an effort to find out where the best research was happening. He came up with a program in Philadelphia where a doctor was having a 70% success rate with his protocol. We told Kathy and her husband and agreed to discuss it with her local oncologist. Her doctor had a high level of respect for this doctor and his program. He suggested we call and get her in his care. It was a sunny Sunday in early spring when he called. The doctor spoke to Kathy and asked her if she wanted to beat this. She giggled with delight as she told him, "Yes, I do." He told her it was imperative that she come with one family member as soon as possible. The doctor asked us to have her records and x-rays sent overnight for his review. The doctor here was extremely cooperative and got the records out. We scurried to get her and her husband on a plane. In little more than 24 hours, they were on a plane, with hope buoyed in our hearts. A 70% success rate! We were going to beat this again! After examining her, the doctor accepted her into his program and started massive doses of chemotherapy with immediate rescue drugs administered to save her from the toxins of the chemotherapy drugs. Her kidneys were continuously monitored for a huge side effect of this drug and the high doses, was kidney failure. The drugs flowed into her for five days and then the waiting began. Daily blood draws to check her white cell count. She could not come home to wait for the next series until her white cell count came back up. She was there about three weeks and came home to celebrate her first Mother's Day and her little sister's graduation from college.

My dancer, my dream
She leaps and she jumps
She is so full of grace
Point, point, tap, tap
On the count of eight
The show is tonight!
The audience arrives
The curtain rises, the music plays
BANG…change of plans
An accident occurs
No show tonight, no dancer's dreams
One small fall, one dream destroyed
Tears and hugs, we love you so
Tomorrow will be another day and another show

I thought my life had changed when Kathy was first diagnosed with the brain tumor, but we adjusted and went on. I thought surely my life had changed when Pat suffered his stroke. What more could God want from me? Now, here I was, with a houseful of family, three brain surgeries between Pat and Kathy, a newborn baby, and a preemie at that! Also throw in one son, who was getting ready to move out in a month because he was to be married in two months and a daughter who was graduating from college. My cup runneth over! Kathy came home in time to go to Colleen's college with us for celebration of the various honors that were being bestowed on her. She was on the Dean's List of Who's Who and was chosen to receive a Dance award. Ceremonies, teas, and chapel services were elegant and allowed us to experience a little bit of the hope we had begun to be afraid to feel. She was rehearsing fiercely, preparing for her final show at school. We were excited with anticipation and allowed hope to creep in again. We were challenging fate but good fortune would come to all of us, and Kathy would be well again and raise her young son. On Thursday, we were able to see part of Colleen's show after the dance awards. Kathy was tired, so we left early to take her and the baby home. I had never missed a performance of Colleen's but that Friday night I was so exhausted, I could not drive to the show. I begged her forgiveness and she told me not to worry. We were coming on Saturday and that would be the better show. About 10:30pm on Friday, the phone next to my bed rang. That lump of fear encroached in my throat. With my heart pounding, I answered the call with trepidation. It was her future mother-in-law, calling to tell me Colleen had been taken to the hospital! She had fallen, just a little bit, but it was bad enough to take her to the emergency room. Pat & I dressed hastily and drove as fast as was safe to the hospital by the college. She fell into my arms in tears, still wearing her costume and stage makeup. It was her ankle and they had x-rayed it. The doctor came in and announced that it was a stress fracture, the kind a dancer fears. Colleen told her to tape it, splint it, whatever, but she was going to dance! They did tape it and put her on crutches. We drove home in a car full of tears. Hopes and dreams......she had worked so hard for four years for this. It was especially hard because it was the summer prior to starting college that Pat suffered his stroke. Her first semester was spent commuting so she could help with her dad. Then Kathy getting sick again, having the baby, it was just too much. We went to a doctor who treats dancers and he agreed it had been the best decision to not dance that night. But believe me, my heart was broken, watching the show that was to be my daughter's, and only seeing her stand-in dance. She cried, I cried, Pat cried, Kathy cried. I was so incredibly proud of her that night. She had worked so hard and accomplished so much. Graduation came two weeks later. I told her it would be best to have a small family gathering at the house to celebrate, of course including her boyfriend, who she had been seeing for over a year. She asked if it would be okay to invite his parents also. Graduation was on Mother's Day. I got up early and prepared Chicken Cacciatore and Veal Parmesan, and set them cooking on time bake in the oven and in the crock-pot. I had a beautiful salad, and different kinds of rolls. I set my best china and crystal out with candles and flowers adorning the table. When everyone was ready, we headed for the college and graduation ceremony. It was a beautiful sunny spring day and the ceremony was outside. It was wonderful to enjoy such a normal occurrence in family life. My daughter was graduating college and I was now a grandmother! After the ceremony, we loaded all cars with her four years of accumulated college stuff and returned home to celebrate.

Dinner at five, don't be late!
The family is gathered, the places are set
Warm food, cold drink. Let us get started
Here's to the future, so big and bright
Here's to us all, together and happy
Dinner at five, don't be late

You may think it odd to devote a chapter to this dinner, but I am sure you will see my reason. You could say I was proud of my cooking and beautiful table. You could say it was because I was so happy to have my family together. However, as you will see.... After cocktails and tidbits, I announced that dinner was ready and everyone began to gather at the table and choose their seats. Even the dog, a big black lab, had settled under the table, dreaming of scraps to come. The last two to sit were Pat and I. As we walked through the door from the kitchen to the dining room, me following Pat, I noticed he was heading a little too far to the left, and of course, he could not realize this. As I reached out to warn him, I realized it was too late. At his left, stood a pagoda style birdcage with two parakeets happily perched inside. His foot clipped the cage, which went flying on its side, brandishing the top across the living room, after which the dog, who was, as you may remember, securely settled under the dining room table, jumped to attention, lifting the entire table with her! As the dog scrambled out to get the birds, whom she had been dying to eat for four years, the birds flew, right back to the table, one of them landing in the Veal Parmesan, and then proceeding to move to the salad plate of Colleen's future mother-in-law, leaving little red footprints on my priceless china. Colleen and Patrick had both jumped to their feet to retrieve the birds and settle the dog. Patrick got the blue bird and set the cage back in position. Colleen caught the yellow one, who was the meanest bird in history and he proceeded to attach his beak to Colleen's hand, causing her to let out a line of expletives, not normally heard from her sweet mouth. I retreated to the kitchen to see what I could salvage and Colleen in her little white dress with her adorable little dancer's figure, came to me and said,"Now what do we do?"Now you must realize, that at this moment, as hectic as it was, on a scale of one to five, having been through brain tumor, stroke, broken bones, and an elderly mother with increasing Alzheimer's, this was not a great concern! I looked at her flatly, and said, "We bring the plates the birds landed on and wash them, give me the meat they walked on, and we resume dinner."We did just that and finally sat down to start our celebratory meal. As I sat down, I looked around the table, ready to start prayers of thanks, when Colleen's future father-in-law looked up and said, "Gee, I didn't know you were going to have entertainment."We cracked up! If you cannot laugh at a time like this, you are in trouble. The laugh was a shot of medicine for us all. We have never forgotten it and enjoy a new laugh every time we think about it. Colleen is married ten years and has two little girls of her own. I hope I will be at their college graduations!

Let me close this chapter by saying that it was a beautiful day for us all, one that brought new hope and good feelings, feelings that perhaps it was okay to dream again, perhaps.

A wedding is coming
A wedding to plan for
A party to have
Engagement
Shower
Shopping and choosing
Gifts of good cheer
A happy time, for sure
A wedding is coming
A wedding, you hear.

It was unbelievable. In January, Kevin was born, in February, Colleen had her senior show, in March, Kevin came home, and Kathy had another brain surgery. In April, Kathy started chemotherapy in Philadelphia. In May, Colleen graduated and Patrick moved into their new home. In June Kathy returned to Philadelphia for chemo and we had a bridal shower for my daughter-in-law. In July, Kathy came home and Patrick was married. It was hard. Nobody denied Pat and his bride their happiness, but she and her family did not understand what we were going through with Kathy. Two things occur when there is serious illness. One is that people avoid you because your misfortune may be contagious, and two is that they blame you for not making the right decisions, which is their reasoning as to why you have suffered such misfortune. It is not malicious, more like denial, or fear of the unknown. While it is extremely hurtful to the victim, it cannot dispose the blame on the offenders. We may all be at that point at one time or another. The treatments were devastating and being on high doses of steroids, her normally delicate features were beginning to balloon, a side effect of the steroids. Her dress had to be altered two sizes prior to the wedding with the increased weight gain. But she was happy. She was looking forward to the wedding, as we all were, and enjoying her baby boy.

Money was becoming an issue. It was hard to work and run my business with all that was going on, and I was losing customers because of it. Every parent wants to give to his or her child at special moments in his or her lives, but it was becoming impossible to do anything. Paying the bills was becoming a bigger and bigger chore. Where were my priorities? I loved my husband, my children, my grandchild, my mother, and I was the major breadwinner. What came first? Priorities were being set minute by minute. I could not worry whether I made the right decision or not, once done, that was it.

The thing I remember most about my son's wedding is being on the dance floor with Pat, looking at each of our children with their significant other, dancing, staring into each other's eyes, hopes, and dreams abounding. I looked at Pat and said,"take a look at the happiness around us…..this may be the last time it will be like this."

It was the last time we would be together to celebrate.

The Kingdom of Magic
A mouse, a duck, a dog
Zippity doo dah
Your dreams will come true
Just wish upon a star
Sprinkle a little fairy dust
And all be well again
A magic place for all to be
Kids once again
Without a care in the world
Mr. Bluebird's on my shoulder
Everything is satisfactory
For now

In August, Colleen went to Florida to work with a very famous mouse. Can you believe? Brain tumor, stroke, and accidents to Mickey Mouse! Is this a weird life or what? She had auditioned for Tokyo Disney and was invited to Florida. Her boyfriend, whom she later married, drove with her to help her get situated. She met two girls, twin sisters who offered to share an apartment with her. They also were employed by the mouse. She worked hard, taking any extra assignments she could get. She worked at Make a Wish breakfasts and greeted the families of the Gulf War soldiers. She auditioned and got a part in the Christmas pageant and parade. She was happy, enjoying tremendous experiences, but getting increasingly homesick, especially for her boyfriend. In November, she begged us to come down for Thanksgiving. It was a tough decision. We were beginning to realize that treatments were not going well. The side effects were massive. Kathy was beginning to hallucinate and was showing the stress of the treatments. The travel and time away from her baby were wearing. We made the very hard decision to drive to Florida to spend Thanksgiving with Colleen. Our reasoning was that we had spent so much time with Kathy in her special moments, that Colleen deserved some attention too. She needed our help and love as much as Kathy did. Therefore, we ensued on our trip, leaving my mother, Kathy, the baby and her husband, to celebrate Thanksgiving alone. Patrick and his wife went to her parents. As much as I dreaded leaving Kathy, by the time we were on the road, I began to enjoy a much-needed relaxation. We drove by our old homes in Indianapolis where we had lived when Colleen was born, and Kathy and Patrick had started school there. Reliving memories as we drove healed a little of the massive hurts we had been through. Just for a little while, we drifted into denial again, remembering the happy times when we were young and the enjoyment of our precious little babies.

That first night, we drove past dinnertime, attempting to make progress on our trip. About 7pm, we made the decision to drive on just a little farther, meeting the travel goals we had achieved on our previous trips. As we settled down to another two hours of travel, the car began a shocking sound of galumphs, galumphs, galumphs. I drifted to the right side of the road and took the next exit. We could not find a service station with a mechanic. There were only gas stations whose sole purpose was to dispense gas. When we checked into the Holiday Inn, we asked for a referral and were told we would have to go back about 100 miles to a major city to find a mechanic. I could not believe it! Short on money, leaving my possibly dying daughter at home, for what could be her last Thanksgiving, and now car problems. Was this God's idea of a joke?

Pat laid his head on the pillow and fell asleep. His logic was and always has been that there is nothing you can do about it now, so you might as well go to sleep. Right, go to sleep, sure. I'll just close my eyes; think sweet thoughts, and presto! Not! Just as in most nights of my life, that night I tossed and turned, wondering what fate would bring us the next day. I had left several messages at Patrick's house, with no return call. I was dismayed. We were in serious trouble and I needed his advice, badly. The next morning, I awoke early to a cloudy, chilly, Thanksgiving Day, high on a mountaintop in Tennessee. I showered, dressed and as I was finishing with my makeup and hair, Pat awoke and started to get ready. I was by now, in worry overdrive. I was going on and on with what will we do, where will we go? What will be open on Thanksgiving Day? Moreover, we only have a week for this little vacation, four days of which are travel there and back. On and on I went, as Pat sat patiently on the bed, listening to me worry and fret. I had short gray, curly hair at the time, which if not conditioned, tended to be wiry and dry. For this purpose I had purchased a hair cream in a blue tube and threw it in with my makeup. As I chattered, I reached for the tube, squeezed some into my hand, and reached up to put it through my hair, not missing a beat or a word. All of a sudden, I stopped, turned, looked at Pat, and said, "I really need this vacation." He sympathetically answered, "I know, we both do." I looked straight at him and said, "No, I REALLY NEED this vacation." As he started again to agree on the justification for our vacation, I showed him the blue tube, out of which I had squeezed a small amount of cream to put in my hair. It was hemorrhoid cream! The distinctive odor caught my attention, thank God! I put the tube down, sat down, and admitted that especially the previous 11 months had taken a toll on my nerves and I REALLY did need this little time off. I tried one more time and reached Patrick, describing the problem. Since he was a mechanic, I thought he would have the answer, which he did. The problem was with some kind of module, which controlled the amount of gas sent to the engine when I stepped on the pedal or something like that. I followed his suggestions and as long as I did not floor the pedal, and kept it even, we had no problems. I have always said that the next best thing to having a son, who is a doctor, is having a son who is a mechanic. I swear mechanics and neurosurgeons follow the same logic when addressing your problem. We spent the remainder of the week with Colleen, not really doing anything special, but just being there, which is what she needed at the time. We shared the warmth of the sunshine and mellow temperatures, which helped to heal some of the stress. We did not really talk much about Kathy. We all knew what we might be facing. It was just not time to confront it.

Soon after Thanksgiving, Kathy had to return to Philadelphia for chemo. It was her eighth trip in as many months. Each visit had become longer than the previous, because her white cell count took longer and longer to rebound. This time, it was much worse. They could not release her with such a low count, because she could so easily catch anything, which could cause devastating side effects. Two days before Christmas, we acknowledged that she would not be home for the holidays, for her son's first Christmas. It was hard on us all. However, I determined to make the best of it. While her husband prepared for the trip to be with her, I put Kevin in his walker and started to bake many of her favorites. Kevin scooted around the kitchen getting into everything. By the end of the afternoon, we were both covered in chocolate and flour, but the treats were ready to go, to give her just a little bit of home for Christmas. We included a few small gifts and sent our love. Christmas day was Pat, Kevin, my mom and me. Patrick and his wife came over early to watch Kevin open his presents before going to be with her family. We all glued our eyes on the television set to see if we could see Colleen in the parade in Florida. We did. We had a star in the family! We called Kathy at the hospital and spoke to Colleen that afternoon. It was a lonely, somewhat fearful Christmas for us all. My mother had traveled with Kathy so much to allow her husband to work and maintain the health insurance. I could take care of the baby and Pat and run my business, which was slowly, but surely slipping into oblivion. It was a good respite for my mom to be at home for Christmas. We felt it important for her husband to be with her in Philadelphia. Kathy was hallucinating badly. She had called me one Saturday morning prior to Christmas. I was changing our bed linens and answered the phone in the bedroom. She was so out of it. I could do nothing but listen and weakly tell her everything would be all right. I cried so hard, I had to get another set of sheets because I had soaked the ones I had. When I hung up the phone, I bowed my head and said, "God, it's obvious that you want her. I cannot see her suffer so. I know you love her and will care of her. I will let her go." Two weeks later, Kathy was released to come home. She arrived on New Year's Eve. Kathy came to us and said she did not want to go back. She had had enough. If she was going to die, that would be it, but she could not continue the stress of the massive doses of chemo and then the rescue drugs. Because of the steroids, she looked nothing like herself. Her beauty had been distorted. Her bright happy eyes now held sadness. They had tried a new treatment they were testing. She and two other young adults were selected for this test. They inserted a tube in the artery in her leg and guided it up to the brain. The problem with treatments had been that the blood brain barrier does not allow the chemotherapy to get to the area of the brain affected by the tumor. It was hoped that this tube would bypass the barrier and get the chemo where it needed to be. In the process of the test, the tube went into some areas it was not supposed to, she was left blind in her right eye, and the chemo did not meet its destination. We felt we must respect her decision, and told her that we would support her in whatever she decided. She called the doctor the next day, and he agreed. She was in the 30% that he was unable to help. The chemo would decrease the size of the tumor, but by the time she returned for the next session, it had grown back to the size it was before. We were not gaining any ground.

Death Be My Friend
No one wants to die
It is inherent to fight
To die is to lose the battle
To give in, to give up
The battle of life
The battle of illness
Die young or old; we fight to the last breath
And when that last breath doth come,
It is our friend….death awaits
The light of life is extinguished
Amen

We celebrated Kevin's first birthday on Kathy's hospital bed, while they were evaluating her condition and attempting to come up with a new treatment plan. The oncologist said he could give some chemo, but it would not do the job. The tumor was resistant and it would survive past the treatment, continuing to cause her problems. It was decided that she go on Hospice, in home. She would die, soon, and at home. The hospice people were wonderful. We got a hospital bed to keep her comfortable. At first, she was able to ambulate and come out for dinner or to watch TV. Then, she began to sleep more and could not sit at the table for more than a few minutes. Holding Kevin, feeding him, became too much and she withdrew from most of that.

While it was hard for each of us, Pat had a very hard time accepting it. He told the hospice psychologist that people do not die at home. They die at the hospital. The doctor firmly, but kindly looked him in the eye and said, "No, Pat, Kathy's going to die at home." We had fought so hard for her survival. Pat had done so much research, looking for the cure, for places to take her where they could help her. If knowledge and positive attitude were the weapons needed, we had been well armed for the battle. People say she lost the battle with cancer. I say she won! She fought a valiant battle, a real Joan of Arc. What I will say next should be accepted carefully. The reason that I say she won is because I believe that it was not in God's plan for her to win. He gave her back to me twice. He did answer my prayers. Nevertheless, in His plan, she was not to live a long life. I have berated myself for everything from perhaps I did not eat well while I was pregnant with her, to perhaps I should have taught her better nutrition, or perhaps we should have found a different doctor. The truth be told, we did everything humanly possible for her. We raised her like a princess and supported her when she grew and went away to college. Easter Sunday, she came out for a few minutes but excused herself to go to bed. As we each said good night to her and then gathered in the living room, it was all too apparent. We were planning for her death. The battle was over.

On April 16, 1991, Kathy succumbed to the tumor, which had ravaged her existence. Quietly, she slipped away. The nurse came out to the kitchen and asked Pat if he wanted to say goodbye. I had run into work, as crazy as it sounds. We had been near this point for so long, I thought I could surely accomplish my tasks and be back in time to say good-bye to my daughter. What was I thinking? How stupid was I? Kathy was not aware, as she had slipped into a semi comatose state days previously. I rushed home to give her a hug, one I had not been able to when she was alive, because she was in so much pain. As we gathered in the living room, the undertaker rolled the gurney past us as we tearfully said goodbye to my firstborn child, my Kathleen.

And this is the end of the story....

Oh Kathy "O"
Oh where is my Kathy?
The one with the bright smile
Oh, my Kathleen
You know what they say about the Irish smile
From little one on
She was oh so happy!
Always able to laugh
Always able to see the bright side
She even laughed at the cancer, she did
She made a little"c"out of the big "C"
She said, "I won't give in"
And she didn't!
She fought, by golly
With a smile on her face and laughter in her voice
She fought with pride
No medal would suffice
She had good times and bad
But then that's the fate of us all
She learned, oh she did
About life and its twists and turns
She learned so early, too early
Where is my Kathleen?
I think I hear a giggle in the air
I think I feel a fresh breeze
I think I found my Kathy "O"
She's all around me, she is!
Happiness is with her, as it always was
The mystery of death, I do not know
But somehow, somehow
I know she is happy and looking down with ease
For she fought, she fought with the best
And she won, don't you know?
She won the battle of life, or can't you see?
A power higher than we

Called her happiness to Him
We had a moment of sparkle in this life with her
But now she fills the sky with stars
Radiating from her precious smile
Resounding from her laughter
A moment, just a moment, please
To listen, to feel, to believe
Do you hear it?
It's my Kathy "O"
From Heaven with love

And this is the beginning....

A new life is begun as
A child is born into this world
A tough little guy is he
His fist as big as my thumbnail
His diminutive body shadowed by the tiny stuffed toy
He eats, he sleeps, and he eats again
One month, two, three, and four
Growing, moving to and fro
The tough little guy grows stronger day by day
He knows not what lies beyond that door
He knows not the sorrow that we feel
Are you my mommy? No, I'm your auntie
Are you my mommy? No, I'm your grand mommy
What has ended in death, begins in life
Her own flesh and blood
God's gift

While my heart ached, there was so much need around me; I did not have time to wallow in my loss. Life was happening in spite of my loss. The day after Kathy's funeral, I wept quietly, while everyone kept to their rooms, each figuratively licking their wounds in their own way. Hospice had kept the house busy with caregivers and respite workers. There were meetings with people from Church to plan the music that would accompany her funeral. Everything came to an abrupt halt as they rolled the gurney with her now lifeless body to the hearse. We had many people back to the house after the funeral but as they left, the silence enveloped us, encouraging us to start the process of letting her go. I was attempting to keep busy with household chores to avoid confronting my feelings. Yet, as I was pushing the vacuum back and forth in the living room, I prayed desperately. "Please God, if I only knew that she was on the other side, that she was safe, please give me a sign." The tears were now streaming down my cheeks as I pushed and pulled, wondering how I would ever live with this broken heart of mine, when I felt a flutter by my right shoulder, and heard a laugh, Kathy's laugh, the one she had when she was younger, a stress free laugh, engaging and playful. I heard her voice say, "Its okay Mom, I'm here, and I'm okay. There's no pain and I'm so happy." Suddenly it all went away, but a tremendous feeling of peace came over me. I stopped, realizing I was in fact alone in the room, no TV, no radio, just me. I felt a lightness take me over. I stopped crying and felt almost joyful! I called Pat and Colleen out of their rooms and told them of my experience. I told them outright that I was sure they would think I was crazy. But I went on to tell them how during this "vision", I saw a bird in this garden, a beautiful garden with flowers of many colors and a brightness beyond belief and an image of Jesus. She was with Him and she was happy and pain free. Before you assume that this woman has lost it, I need to tell you what occurred several years later. Someone had suggested I read a book about guardian angels. I do not remember the name of the book or the author. It related several stories about people who had encountered angels, and their almost unbelievable stories. The one that struck me was a woman who related an "out of body" experience who described following the light to a garden, where Jesus was waiting for her. She described the garden in detail. I gasped as I read for she described the garden that I had seen Kathy in.

During her illness, Kevin had become the child to everyone. He had friends and family and neighbors all rooting for him. He could not fall down without having someone there to whisk him up. He seldom cried, always took things in stride, and grew stronger each day. As he toddled around trying his first steps, he would suddenly lose it and fall down. "Touch down" he would say. He had been influenced by watching football with Boppy (Pat) and was very interested in the football players falling down. He would hear Pat yell "touch down" and picked up the phrase. From the tiny little babe whose fist was no larger than my thumbnail, he grew.

By the time he turned his second year, he was considerably closer to normal size. He began speaking in simple sentences when he was only one year old. He was a delightful baby, never showing the tremendous stresses going on around him. He never fussed at who was holding him, which made for pleasant visits from his mom, when she was alive, who had oh so little time to hold him and love him. There is no scale to measure, but I am confident that the bond between mother and child existed and grew even though their meetings grew farther and farther apart.

When we entered into hospice, we had a family meeting with the psychologist who helped us to address the reality of impending death. As we gathered in our living room with the entire family, Kevin, who was now attempting to walk, moved about the coffee table in front of the sofa, with a napkin in hand, cleaning and polishing the table. It was a most solemn meeting, each of us addressing our fears and announcing our acceptance of reality. It was with heart in my throat that I listened to my daughter say that she was going to die. She did not want to. She would have fought if the battle were fair, if the weapons were ones she could use effectively. However, she realized, more than we did, that it was time. What is that poem? A time to laugh, a time to cry, a time to live, and a time to die. In this most serious moment, as this happy little child scooted around the table, a burst of laughter pealed through the room as we all, for a bit, enjoyed the very normal activities of a one year old. But that is the way Kevin has always been, and that is the way Kathy was, a wonderful sense of humor and the ability to make others laugh.

The day she died, we could not hug him enough as we all sought the consoling aura of a one year old to help ease our pain of loss. Could anyone ever replace Kathy in my heart? Absolutely not. But she had left this gorgeous part of her, a testimony to her being. Life quickly became an adjustment to reality. The needs of my husband, my mother, my son-in-law, and Kevin were my priorities. My business bumped along but I was losing accounts because I could not devote the time needed on the customers. We began to enjoy every moment of Kevin. What one year old does not engage your senses? We began to take him to the zoo, museums, take walks, read books and play. He was a good and loving child. I was ever so aware that biologically, and legally, his father should be the primary caregiver. However, day after day, our concern grew as he showed the lack of skills needed to parent a young child. We never questioned his love for Kevin. He actually came to me and told me he would not know what to do if he were on his own. There was no way he would be able to care for Kevin himself. Alternatives? His family, where not one of them had proven they could even handle their own lives, let alone that of a tiny child, or he could get married again. We knew this was probably what the future held. I even encouraged him to date. We could not foresee that he would marry someone who was less capable than he to parent a child. While they lived with us, we all tried to encourage his father, to teach him, and to help him to prepare for his parental role, but nothing improved. Kevin began to be the leader in this strange father/son relationship. As he grew, Kevin would create the imaginary games, relegating roles to his father. He had one favorite game at the time, naming it after a toy his father had bought him. They were called Crash Dummies. They came with cars that the child could crash, and the dummies would fall apart. A sick concept when you think about it, but they were trying to encourage children to use seat belts by using these toys. In Kevin's imaginary game, he posed his father as a crash dummy and went about with the play. We tried to tell Kevin it was not nice to call anyone a dummy, but there was no sense of reality from the parent as he went along with the play. Later, the psychologist told us that when she saw the parent and child together, it was as if the roles were reversed. Kevin would take the lead and tell his father what they should be doing. Meanwhile, in an effort to expose Kevin to the many opportunities for learning, we increased our outings to the various zoos, museums, and movies. We had some exciting adventures, searching the zoo for Elihu the Musical Gnu Who Lived in the Zoo and Played a Kazoo"(by Hannah Simons, illustrated by Molly Kinsley) One day we went deep into the coal mine at the museum to ride the coal train. A child's imagination could easily believe that he was riding the ghost train that raced through the dark, dark tunnel that we had read about. I read a lot to Kevin. When we were not reading, he had a tape player and books. Every night after we read his bedtime story, he would climb into his bed, turn on his tape recorder and follow the story in his book until he fell asleep. We had books on tape to listen to in the car. As he grew older, we moved into some of the classics. By the time he was first tested, he was reading four years above his grade level. Even at a young age, taking him to the library was an adventure. When he was about one and a half, we started to introduce him to the concept of potty training, placing a potty chair in the bathroom, anticipating the urges and reading the new array of potty training storybooks available. However, every night when his father came home, he reversed our efforts and told Kevin, "You don't have to do it if you don't want to." We urged him to work with us to make it easier on Kevin. He firmly stated that someone had told him that when Kevin was five, he would automatically know what to do and therefore we did not need to work with him. He could wear diapers until then. Anyone who has had a growing toddler remain in diapers too long knows all too well the odor and frequent rashes and sores that begin to occur, almost signaling the time for the child to be using the toilet. The fact eventually became known when he finally realized that Kevin could not participate in any of the park district programs available if he was not toilet trained. Screech! Put on the brakes! Now we go in reverse and attempt to teach the child again! Of course, by now, Kevin was resistant to the efforts even though his father began to support us. Pat spent time daily helping Kevin with this chore but Kevin was not fully trained until he was 4 years old. We maintained a low-key approach with a steady pace to teach the child that it was now okay to use the toilet. Of course, what does a child do in confused surroundings? He runs, and he did, every time potty was spoken. Feeling that there was still hope now that his father had finally agreed to work with us and not against us, we edged forth with a positive attitude.

On a lovely day in spring, we spent the day at the museum where he would have the freedom to explore and test all the various exhibits. Patiently, each time we passed a restroom, we would ask, "Do you have to go? Do you want to try?" "NO, I don't have to!" was the continuous response. At the end of the day, we paused for a short while to allow him to play in the developmental playroom. I trailed him around the room, never losing sight of him. After trying all the puzzles, blocks, drawings and climbing the ladders, going down the slide and playing with the miniature fire hoses, he agreed to leave. The museum was closing as we left a long adventure into play and imagination. As we walked to the car, he stopped, stamped his foot, and said, "you need to take me back…you need to change my pants….I poopied in my pants!" I patiently told him, "I'm sorry but they have closed and locked the doors. The museum is now closed. We will have to change you when we get home." He was furious! He was becoming aware of the discomfort, which accompanied not using the toilet. Who could blame him? He was getting conflicting messages at home. We got in the car, seat belts in place, and headed for home. The lovely spring sunshine streamed rays through the car windows. Kevin, in the back seat, was unusually quiet. He always had a comment about something! All of a sudden, the tiny voice of the three year old came from the back, "I'm really mad at you guys!" We both said, "We asked you many times to go to the bathroom and you refused to even try. I'm sorry if you're uncomfortable, but that's why I wanted you to try." He simmered for a few moments, silence again filling the car. Then, out of the depths of the back seat, the tiny voice came again, "Well, I'm going to go home and my daddy's going to clean me up and put powder on my bottom so it won't get sore." I said, "Well, that's fine, but what about tomorrow? The reply was precious! "Don't you worry about tomorrow; I'll just use my Depends." As we burst out laughing, we realized the true confusion this child must be going through. I had my mother who was 80 and wearing depends and a 3 year old wearing Pampers. Many times, he would shop with Colleen or me as we purchased these items for both ends of the spectrum. How confusing it must have been for him! If you do it when you are a baby and when you are old, what is the big deal? He was cleaned up when we got home and toilet training efforts improved from then on. It would have been so much easier to have his father work with us. Three years of age was not too early to work on potty training.

He excelled in various preschool programs. His father seldom took part in any of the preschool activities. If a parent was needed to help, attend a conference, or watch a skit, it was Pat and I, or Colleen who would be there. His father refused to be involved and never encouraged anything Kevin learned. It was sad, but we filled the gaps where we could, hoping that the arrangement would work for Kevin. He was so incredibly sweet! When he was not yet two, he started to greet me as "daidy" for Daisy Duck because of the hat I wore when we played. He would help me make the bed and we played parachute with the bed sheets, singing the Mickey Mouse Club Song…. "Forever let us hold our banner high," stretching our arms to the sky. He would go to Pat as he dressed, helping him with his leg brace, closing the Velcro closure for him. Then he would go to Colleen's room, "Coween, Coween, wake up Coween!" He had indeed taken hold of our hearts. As he started preschool, he started to call Colleen Mom. She told him, "I'm not your mom, I'm your auntie, and I love you very much." He came to me and asked if I was his Mom. I said, "No I'm your grand mommy". We showed him pictures of Kathy, told him this was his mom, who loved him very much, but could not stay with him. Of course, this was too much for a young child to grasp, but we had to give the best answers possible. The bonds were growing. We talked it over and decided to go to the cemetery to visit Kathy's grave, as a family. We took flowers and Kevin took a balloon to send up to heaven. We tried to answer questions the best we could and keep a positive twist as much as possible. There is no right way to do this sort of thing. When Kevin was tested at age three, as a follow up to his preemie status, he was found to have the vocabulary of a four and a half-year-old. He was using words not normally known at his age like "substantial." His sentences were well structured and communication was extremely effective. He would greet Colleen's boyfriends at the door, inviting them in with, "Hi, come on in and take your coat off. Do you want something to drink?" His comfort level with all ages became apparent. He could cozy up with my mother at 80, play with other children his age, or converse with adults, always inquisitive as to the why's and wherefore's of everyone. It remained evident that it was a necessity for us to be involved in Kevin's parenting. His father seemed eager to take on the role, but consistently showed he lacked the interest or skills necessary. We were ever aware that no matter what we thought, or how we felt, the biological father had the rights and if we were to maintain a relationship with our daughter's child, we could not take the parent role from his father. We ensued on the path of least resistance and continued to work with his father, hoping he would learn and eventually take over the parental role. What one must understand is that this man came from a home unlike most others, where parenting skills were totally lacking and socially unacceptable behavior was considered the norm. I will not go into particulars but every professional involved had expressed concern about Kevin's future with his father. His extreme facial ticks, distorted speech, and gross lack of coordination were questioned by everyone who met him. The questions were asked. Did he have MS? Did he have Tourett's? I could not answer their concerns. I did not know. The physical problems coupled with the lack of skills emotionally brought concern to everyone. The extended family had significant problems of their own and therefore were of no help.

When Kevin was three and after many conversations with friends, family and professionals, I sat his dad down to talk about his symptoms. I suggested that for Kevin's sake, it would be a good idea to look into the reason for these symptoms. So far, he and his family did not notice a problem, in spite of the many questions from everyone involved in his life. Believe me, this was not the position I wanted to be in. The only motivating force for me was Kevin. If this was something genetic, it needed to be diagnosed. The paternal grandparents had never addressed the symptoms exhibited by their son. I explained that if it was something hereditary, we should know, for Kevin's sake. He agreed and found a neurologist who diagnosed a rare genetic disorder. He was given Botox treatments for a while, to ease the obvious facial tics, but he did not want to continue with them. When Kevin was eight, we had him evaluated by a pediatric neurologist. He found Kevin without any signs of this syndrome, and stated his father was in the top 25% of the worst cases. It proved to be the right decision to approach him because some of the information he found from testing later helped Kevin's doctor when he was 16, in treating him.

A typical day for Kevin was for his dad to get him up, sit him in front of the TV with a bowl of dry cereal, and proceed to ready himself for work. He would just leave, not even making sure that one of us was up and knew what to do with Kevin. Either Colleen or I would take Kevin to the toilet, wash him, dress him, and get him a balanced breakfast. Then his day could start. He was still small and needed adequate nourishment and to be taught daily living skills. He was only two when we discussed his need to be with other children and decided to place him in part time daycare. Kevin suffered a tremendous amount of separation anxiety, as I would drop him off. Because of schedules, I always took him and picked him up. He would cry and beg me not to leave him. He had a very good teacher and I knew he must learn so I would tell him I loved him and told him that he never needed to worry, that "Daisy" would always be there. It was what I had done for my children and now was doing it again for my daughter's child. It was so hard....I would leave the daycare after reassuring him and I would break down in tears in the car, telling my husband, "I'm not supposed to have to do this." Every time I would pick him up, I would reassure him that, "See, I told you I'd come back and I did." These words, these actions, would come back to haunt me in a few years.

During this time also, with my mother's deteriorating memory, I placed her in an adult day care. Therefore, my day would consist of taking her to her daycare, then taking Kevin to his daycare, and then running to my office and trying to run a business until it was time to do the reverse route. I would arrive at adult day care first, trying to urge my mother on so I could get to Kevin's daycare to pick him up. A few times as I was trying to rush her out, I forgot about the bracelets the patients wore to avoid anyone leaving the facility and roaming the streets unattended. The alarm would go off; we would have to back up and wait for someone to take the bracelet, get her in the car, and then off to get Kevin. First, you cannot rush an elderly person, no matter how hard you try and if you do, it is bordering on being cruel. So the finesse of urging her on as quickly as possible became a skill I did not know I had. From Kevin's daycare, it was home to prepare dinner for everyone, do some household chores, and catch up on a few phone calls while trying to plan for the next day. I let his father take over in the evening with getting Kevin ready for bed. I would read a book to him at some time during the evening and his father would put him in front of the TV and sit with him while he watched the same video night after night. I kept reminding myself that I must keep my place that I should not step in and hoped that his father would soon learn some skills, a hope that proved to be fruitless.

Kevin began to get sinus and ear infections. After he got it, we got it, one by one. By the time it was finished going around, he would start again. One night everyone in the house was coughing and sneezing and I said, "That's it, I'm taking him to the pediatrician tomorrow". I did, and the doctor told me that statistically, an average two year old in day care gets an average of twelve upper respiratory infections per year. Well we were right on as it took about a month for it to go through the house before we started all over again. When I got home from the doctor, I said, "Can we afford to have this child in daycare?" We were all missing work because of being sick. So we went to plan B. Colleen was piecing her life together, working part time as a dance teacher and part time as a manicurist. She loved Kevin dearly and volunteered to pitch in again. She would care for him in the morning if I could take him in the afternoon. Since he napped in the afternoon, I could get some work done. It was a good experience for Kevin. Colleen had an upbeat personality that was good for him. She easily taught him daily skills; ones that his father did not even exercise himself, let alone know how to teach the child. I would get him in the afternoon and work from home while caring for him, preparing dinner, doing laundry, etc, etc.

As my mother's memory worsened, she became defensive. She would come home, eat dinner, and go to her room, taking the dog with her to share the multiple pieces of toasted bread she would munch on every night. She began to be paranoid, accusing me of being "out to get her."Eventually, I took her to a psychiatrist for treatment who said,"There's nothing wrong with her, she's just trying to find more ways to bug you." He started her on some medication, which helped greatly, and we went on trying to maintain some normalcy in our lives. Days ran into weeks, months, and so on as it goes. I had started working a couple of nights per week and alternate weekends at the hospital so I could get health insurance for Pat and me. Our household took on a somewhat discombobulated schedule, with work, childcare, elder care, and general household duties filling the hours and days.

I worked on rebuilding my business. I was filled with joy and anticipation at the opportunities afforded me, but always, the sadness loomed as a cloud over my head. No joy that Kevin gave us could overcome the loss of Kathy. I kept busy enough to avoid confronting that loss, to avoid facing the realty that Kevin and his dad may someday move on. I could only hope that it would be a smooth transition. I prayed to God for no more loss, please, no more loss. I rebuilt my business to a point, but never could regain the energy I had when I first started it. Three brain surgeries between Kathy and Pat, and the loss of Kathy was just too much. I felt like I had been kicked in the stomach and pushed in a hole and I was desperately trying to catch my breath and claw my way out. I began to have anxiety attacks, though I managed to cover them up and forced myself to regain control. I could not afford the luxury of losing control, of getting sick, of needing a hug, or just an easy night of fun. Too many people were depending on me. Colleen always tried to help and did what she could, but she was at an age where she was trying to start her own life and the struggling conflicts were taking their toll on her. Life went on this way for four years. Kevin had determined that I was his Daisy. When Pat would call me at the hospital after dinner on the nights I worked, he would put Kevin on the phone to say goodnight and Kevin would say, "Daisy, come out of the phone, come out of the phone now." I laughed at these precious moments until I cried. The medicine of laughter began to heal the hurt. I could hear Kathy's laughter in him. Life goes on and time heals, not completely, but enough for you to go on.

Kevin's dad started to go out with a woman. It was almost three years after Kathy's death and we anticipated he would go on with his life and probably get married again. It was not talked about, but when he brought her to meet us and told us of their plans to live together, I just asked that we be able to maintain a relationship with Kevin. He assured me there would be no problem, and I believed him.

You saved me from the monsters!
Life goes on
The sun rises and sets
It pays no attention to the hurts and joys we encounter
It still rises and sets
It still maintains its' beauty
Our hopes are renewed with each day
Worry and Peace play in our minds
Which will it be today?
Life is changing and we must move on
Happier things are sure to come
BANG…life changes
The monsters in the closet have escaped and are attacking
Too little to fight, he needs help
"You saved me from the monsters!"
What job have I been given?
No Joan of Arc am I!
How do I save the little babe?
The monsters are threatening
I cannot ignore him….I must do something
Please God, a plan, a plan, I need help!

In August of Kevin's fourth year, he and his dad moved in with his new wife and her son who was three years older than Kevin was. They had been married secretly in the court. Why secretly, no one knew. No one begrudged him his happiness and a normal family environment would be good for Kevin. We looked forward to taking the grandparent role. Normal is the operative word. Meetings with his new wife proved to be more bizarre each time we met. Each time we saw Kevin, he was dirty and smelled of cheap aftershave, which she had splashed on him to cover the body odor. His fingernails were dirty and his hair was plastered down with greasy dirt. Always being a gregarious child, and excited to see us, he would start getting excited, talking, and laughing. Her reaction to this was to immediately reprimand him, stating he was not listening and he was being very bad. Her repeated rebukes were met by confusion on Kevin's part. He had always been a good child and redirection was all he ever needed. She refused to find a way to deal with him. She gave him repeated time outs, one after the other, five minutes, and then 10 minutes until we were rapidly approaching an hour of time outs for a child who was too young to understand the concept. He also could not see what he was doing wrong. We found out later that the time outs became locking him in his room all afternoon, sending him to bed without dinner, and washing his mouth with soap. While the honesty of children is sometimes alarming, his comments about her cooking were met with a childish anger on her part. She would send his dad to hit him with his belt, lock him in his room and eventually started giving him a spoonful of hot sauce if he would not eat. She even carried a bottle in her purse for use in restaurants. Kevin began to resist eating, making food his battleground. Within six weeks after moving, his dad announced that we could no longer see Kevin. When we asked why, he had no reason, just that they had decided and that was it. It was crushing, not only to us, but we knew the turmoil Kevin must be in because of our close relationship. It was I who had assured him I would always be there. It was Pat who had toilet trained him and watched football. It was Colleen who would be there in the morning with him, lovingly fixing him toasted waffles with sprinkled powdered sugar. Either Colleen or I would take him to preschool, read him books, and teach him things like making cookies, playing with blocks and all of the other important activities that children learn by. I had spoken with his father when he announced they would be moving and he promised that we would always have a relationship with Kevin. This promise was not true. Kevin had been enrolled for the fall in the preschool he had been attending in the spring. He had done so well, we all hoped he would continue. He needed to learn social skills by being with his peers. However, all of these things were put aside when the battles began. We contacted a lawyer regarding grandparent's visitation rights. The lawyer got us those rights, after $10,000 in fees. Then the games began. There was not a visit without an occurrence. We had to accept supervised visitation at first. We had to take him to a public place to visit. Usually we went to the indoor mall where he could safely run around and we could have dinner. He missed everyone, was worried about his toys that were left behind and worried about his dogs, Sami and Lady, a pug and a black lab. He begged to go to our house to see them. We could not take him. Upon return from visitation, we were greeted with rudeness and sarcasm. One time I was followed down the sidewalk with his stepmother screaming at me, and when I turned to her, I thought for sure she was going to hit me. This was all because we had not said goodbye to her. We were under lawyer's orders to avoid any confrontation with this crazy woman…just pick him up, visit, and take him back. We always said our goodbyes before he got out of the car to avoid any scenes.

One Saturday, we picked up Kevin and were to drive out to see the house that Colleen's fiancé had bought for them. We arrived to pick Kevin up and his dad was standing there, kind of weird. I stepped out of the car and his dad told Kevin to go ahead. I opened the back door and he got in and sat quietly while I secured him in his seatbelt. As I got into the car, his dad stood and stared. Kevin began to kick and scream, "I don't want to go with you, I hate you, you're the cause of all the problems, Kathy's not my mom." We had asked the court to appoint a lawyer to protect Kevin's rights and she had explicitly told us that if anything like this occurred, we were just to go on and complete out visit. She was experienced in this and saw it coming. We had not, and we were shocked. For twenty minutes, Kevin went on saying, "I hate you, you're the cause of the problems, it's all your fault, I hate you, I want to kill you, I want to kill you with a knife." After about 20 minutes, I pulled into a gas station and stopped the car. There was an uneasy silence. My voice drifted to the back seat. "Are you finished?" A quiet "yes" was the response. I turned to him and said, "I'm sorry you hate us, we love you." His worried little face screwed up tearfully and he said, "I love you too." The rest of the visit was uneventful and we had a good time, but the stress was there and could not be ignored.

We arranged to take him to the Historical Museum to see the dinosaurs for another visit. We arrived to pick him up and found no one at home. We waited, we called, and we knocked, and finally, on lawyer's orders, went to the police station to make a report. We had to follow the officers back and wait while they attempted to call and go to their door, only to find that the father had taken Kevin to a museum, even though it was our court ordered visiting time. The visits became more tense. On and on it went. We never knew what to expect, but were painfully aware of the toll it was taking on Kevin. Mother's day we went to breakfast. We were 10 minutes late in returning and his dad was standing on the drive accusing us of deliberately being late. His wife had tried to stop the mother's day visit, stating that our plans were to take him to the cemetery. The few visits that Kevin was with us to the cemetery were uneventful. He would happily send his balloon to Heaven to Mommy. We stayed barely five minutes each time. I think Kevin had been at the cemetery twice. We always had kept the attitude that Kathy was his mom, loved him very much, but God wanted her to be with Him. Simple and to the point.

We asked why he was not attending preschool, when the follow-up clinic for preemies had recommended that he needed to attend preschool. We offered to take him and pick him up if that was a problem. The stepmother said she would enroll him, but he went one time and that was the end of the that. As the stress increased and the police became more involved, attorney fees escalated and the stress was tearing us apart. We just wanted to be involved with our daughter's child and we did not want to just drop him after being so involved in his early childhood. He needed a transitional time with all adults working closely together to make it happen. Dealing with two very dysfunctional adults, each of whom were exhibiting serious mental problems, and absolutely no parenting skills, prohibited this from ever happening. It became a power struggle, though we had no power. The law provided us with visitation, but they were not about to allow that to happen. They wanted a fight. They were also running up lawyer bills but had no intention of paying them. They had planned a huge wedding in a church with a big reception, gowns, tuxedos, flowers, et al. Where the money was coming from for all of this was the question. We found out later that she had run up all of his charge accounts and expected the guests to pay for everything. Surprise!

We went on with our lives, enjoying what we could with visitation. I still had my mom to care for and Colleen was moving towards her engagement and wedding preparations. Our son Patrick was now married and we saw little of him, as he moved on with his life. It was a frustrating time, because Kevin would always ask us to take him home with us, to see the dogs, to see Colleen, and we had to tell him we could not. "Why" was not a question we could answer in a way a child could understand. There were no real reasons, just fabricated ones from two so-called adults who were not handling their own lives, let alone that of a child. The only outlet Kevin had was his relationship with her son. Kids have a way of bonding together during hard times. They were both frequently locked in the bedroom or stayed there out of fear as the parents fought and screamed at each other. While she was screaming to the court about the bond she had formed with Kevin, Kevin's hatred for her grew. He would proudly tell us how he would not eat her "dog food"and had to take a spoonful of hot sauce because he would not. He told us of the night that his dad "almost put her head in the fish tank."The stepmother began to complain that Kevin had diarrhea after our visits. She claimed she talked to the doctor and it was because our visits were upsetting him. She neglected to include the hours before the visit when she prepared him, telling him what to say, what to think, what to do. Calls to children and family services were met with rudeness and we were told to mind our own business. Their announced visit to the house brought exactly what was planned. The children were coached and instructed on what to say. The caseworker did not care, because it just was not important enough in comparison to the severity of most cases they see. Kevin told us the whole story about the visit and what they were told to say. It had been over a year of turmoil, mostly for Kevin. It was hard on us, but it was devastating to him. His dad and stepmother, nor the paternal grandparents could see that. They tugged and they pulled at him relentlessly, accusing him of loving us, telling him his mother never existed, telling him they were the only important ones. It was painful to witness and the inability to change anything was frustrating to say the least. I went on about my work and caring for my husband and my mother. The sad reality however was that Kevin needed a mother, and when his dad remarried, his wife was the least likely candidate to mother anyone. Her mental stability was lacking and she was histrionic, constantly causing simple events to become catastrophic.

After months of court visits and rulings. Kevin was showing signs of mayhem. The lawyers were getting concerned. His dad was on his third lawyer, walking away as soon as he ran up a bill he never intended to pay. The new wife had run up all of his credit cards with the big wedding, the furniture, honeymoon, etc. and he was now broke. He never had much of a job and he was plagued with his wife and mother calling him at work and bosses who were losing their patience with him. The symptoms of the syndrome he suffered from were getting worse. The battles and staged confrontations at every visitation were wearing us down. Police reports were adding up, but to what avail? We just wanted to visit with him. We planned fun things. They accused us of trying to replace our daughter with him. The stepmother's histrionics were upsetting Kevin and us. Kevin would run to the bathroom stating that he had diarrhea again. He stated his stepmother told him it was because we were visiting with him. I raised three kids and worked in a hospital for five years. I knew what diarrhea looked like. His bowel movements were soft and light colored, not green and foul smelling. I believe she was feeding him mineral oil to produce what she thought would look like diarrhea. On each visit, he was badly in need of a bath. He was now afraid to do things. If I asked him if he wanted strawberries, which I knew he loved, he would say, "No," to which I would say, "Okay, I thought you liked strawberries." He would then go into, "No, you don't understand; yes means no and no means yes."

"So you want strawberries."

"No". I would give him the strawberries and he would say, "That's right," and devour the strawberries. His dad and stepmother decided they were going to adopt each other's child, which normally would be good. However, she made it quite clear to the lawyers that when she adopted Kevin, she would say whom he would see, and it definitely would not be us. Abuses increased. The hot sauce and beatings continued. Kevin grew tough and firmly stated they could not hurt him. Time outs grew in number and many times lasted all night, with no dinner. It was still questionable why they were continuing on this path of destruction. We never challenged them nor demanded custody. We merely said we wanted to be involved in Kevin's life in some way. She put Kevin on a fat free diet and he was losing weight. We thought he was attending school and saw that as an improvement as he would be with other children. We found out that she took him once and never returned. He started kindergarten in September of his 5th year. We did not know until later, that she had been keeping him out of that school also. By mid October, he had been in school a total of 10 days.

One quiet Sunday night, as we were relaxing in our living room, the phone rang and it was the paternal grandfather, screaming and yelling at me. It turned out that Kevin's dad had been taken to the hospital with chest pains and while they were in the ER, the wife began to complain that she had a heart condition and that it was all due to the stress we were causing. She neglected to tell them of the continuous stress she put on every one in her life, including her husband, children, and us. They were both released. No heart attacks, just hysterics. We had no qualms about what our role was. We just wanted visitation. We did not spend any time telling Kevin anything but that we loved him and let us have fun while we are together. This had been going on almost a year. We had moved into visitation at our home, which was great for Kevin especially. He played with the dogs and just had a relaxing few hours without anyone fighting or screaming at him, or telling him what to do or say. It was always hard when it was time to take him back. He begged not to go. We had to tell him we must, but that things would get better, a promise we hoped we would be able to keep, but the prospects were poor. Later, when Kevin was eight, this came back to haunt us. One night, Kevin was upset over some little thing. I asked him why he would not trust us. His response, "You took me back to them," referring to the visitations when he begged us to take him home with us.

We had the opportunity to travel with a group from Colleen's dance studio to Disney World for a long weekend. We asked for permission at the court and it was granted. His dad and stepmother reluctantly agreed when the judge said he could see no harm in it. Again, Kevin's attorney was ahead of the game and asked for a status hearing the Monday before (we were to leave on Thursday morning and asked to pick him up on Wednesday night because of our early departure). We showed up in court on Monday, they did not. The judge asked their attorney where they were. He stated he did not know. The judge ordered us all back in court the next morning. The next morning brought all of our fears to a summit. Their lawyer stated that per the stepmother, "The father bolted with the kid."Why? A trip to Disney World? Five days? What could be the problem? The judge had allowed Pat not to come that day so I was the only one there. I was escorted to a police car and we embarked on a search of their home, the entire area, etc. to no avail. That night another squad car picked up Pat and I and we again searched locations where they might be. We ended up at the paternal grandparent's house where the police determined that they knew where he was at but would not cooperate. This was Tuesday. By Wednesday night we were beside ourselves with worry. What kind of lunatics were we dealing with? The lawyer said we could not leave, because if they found Kevin, we would have to return home immediately to pick him up. So with tearful goodbyes, I saw Colleen off to Disney World. We had anticipated this trip to be one of enjoyment. Now, we were carrying the pain of worry in our hearts. What had he done with Kevin? We went into the office, trudging through the day the best we could. About 12:30, we received a call that they had found them and they were downtown. We needed to get down there as soon as possible. We tore out of the office and arrived at the court to meet our attorney. They had put his father in jail and Kevin was with the sheriff. The stepmother sat across the aisle with her friend and kept leering at us and sticking her tongue out. The father was brought before the judge and asked about his rights. The judge immediately gave temporary custody of Kevin to us! The lawyers had all warned us that there was no way we would ever get custody, yet here we were. We went with our lawyer to the sheriff's office to pick up Kevin. The sheriff came out and spoke to the stepmother and us. She expressed a great concern about what all of this was doing to Kevin. She was right. There was no disagreement on our part; we knew it was tearing him up. He did not know who to love, who to trust, or who would take care of him. He was only five years old! Our attorney was concerned for our safety after witnessing the actions of the stepmother and her friend, so she took Pat and Kevin back to her office while I got the car. As her assistant helped them into the car and we pulled away, the silence was crushing, the fears of a little child hung in the air. The first words out of his little mouth were, "I don't care what you say; I'm not going to eat." He was dressed in clothes that were torn and at least a size too small. His little sneakers with the action figures on them were torn and soiled. He was dirty, he was scared, but he was not hungry. Food had become his battleground. He weighed 30 lbs with his clothes on and he was almost six years old.

When we had called the airline to inform them we would not be on our flight, they instructed us to call as soon as we had the child and we would be on the next flight. We left for Disney World that Friday morning to catch up with the group. Every mother gasped at his thinness and circles under his eyes. Most of them had known him for most of his young life and could not believe how he looked. He loosened up. We had bought some clothes for the trip so we were prepared with that. The first night we were there, he begged to order a pizza from room service, jumping happily on the big bed. The pizza came quickly, but he was fast asleep, having just collapsed on the bed moments before. His eyes were wide and excited, but with a pain glowing behind them. The aura of the Magic Kingdom brought weakened smiles to his face. It was very hot that October and one evening we decided to break away from the crowd and allow him to take a swim at the hotel pool. While he swam, I went in and bought hamburgers for our poolside dinner. When I approached the pool, my spirits leapt as I watched him joyfully splash and play with the other children. I got him out of the pool and toweled him off as he dove for the chair and bit off a huge bite of hamburger. He gleefully announced that it was the best hamburger her had ever had and ravenously devoured it with the accompanying French fries. To this day, we will look at each other and say, "Remember the hamburger at the hotel pool?" On the day we were to return home, they had pictures of the father and stepmother on the front page of the local newspaper, crying because we were trying to steal their son. We wanted to have visitation.

We wanted to be involved in our grandson's life in some small way. We were fighting against their continual efforts to take away our visitation rights. Our goal was to help Kevin transition into his new life. We had been his primary caregivers and just snatching him away was destructive for him. They went on to hire a lawyer who had the story at the top of the news every 30 minutes for two days until the judge ordered it stopped. We had reporters calling and coming to our office, who were eager to make a big story of this. We just wanted to be grandparents. We did not kidnap him. We took him to Disney World and brought him home as planned.

We made every attempt to settle into a quiet life. Kevin needed to have as little turmoil in his life as possible. I needed to get him eating again, and enjoying it. Kevin continued in his original school, per court order, to maintain some semblance of normalcy. It was tough, knowing the school was about six miles away while we had one that was in the same district just one block away. We also knew how important it was to comply with the court orders so we proceeded in our new agenda of being parents, not grandparents again.

The first day I took him to school, I was taken aback as the teacher barked at me that it would just be wonderful if he came to school every day. We did not know that the stepmother had been keeping him home. It was almost the third week in October and he had barely completed one week of school. I assured her he would be there. Knowing what kind of dramatics the stepmother had caused, I arrived at the school to pick him up later that day, standing in line with the young mothers, wondering if I would be attacked for being the "wicked grandmother". To my surprise, most people did not even notice me, and one kind lady approached me and introduced herself, stating, "I knew there was another side to the story…this must have been so hard on you." A friend in need is a friend indeed. We went on to meet and talk frequently as we waited for the children. We were able to keep Kevin involved with his schoolmates and he quickly was accepted and invited to play dates and birthday parties. It was always with fear that I would drop him off for one of these activities, not knowing if the stepmother had planned something to interfere with it. My fears were relieved as Kevin began to build friendships and play like any other kid. Schoolwork, even for kindergarten, was hard for him. Since she had kept him out of preschool, he had missed many skills the other children had developed. Fortunately, his gregariousness kept him socially up to par. The signs of trouble were his acting out behavior and were especially evident in the pictures he drew at school. They were making journals and each day she asked him to draw a picture of the sun, a bird, mom, dad, brother, sister, etc. He would bring the journal home at the end of the week and we would review the days and the drawings, all scribbled in black crayon. I remember one picture that was supposed to be of a family outing, Mom, Dad and children. He covered the page in black crayon. We ensued on teaching him his letters and offering various colors of crayons to portray his pictures. He was six years old by then and he could not even draw a stick figure. It was not until second grade that he began to draw stick figures and not until third grade that he added features like eyes. It always amazed me as he got older and teachers frequently criticized his drawings and his inability to complete a paper. They just would not listen when I told them how far he had come in such a relatively short time. He did not fit into the norm nor did he fit into special education criteria. Efforts to communicate with teachers to understand Kevin's problems always ended with no results. They would always say, "Well, that was a long time ago."Yes, it was, but the scars were there and would need to be dealt with, better sooner than later. We saw the school social worker, who was in a tremendous hurry to have him diagnosed ADHD and put on medication. They had us view a video regarding this subject. However, we were still traveling a distance to see the psychologist from the court who wanted to continue to help him through the transition of change. We told her of the school's concern and she told us he was not ADD or ADHD, but he did have issues from what he had been through. We returned the videos and told them, "Please do not insult our intelligence again with this subject. We have spoken to the psychologist and she says Kevin in NOT ADHD! However, he does have baggage from his tumultuous past that needs to be dealt with." We would not put him on pills because they could not find a way to teach him! Of course, this did not make us popular.

Kevin had been having increased sinus infections and ear infections. We were becoming regulars at the pediatrician's office. We had taken him in October to have him checked out. He was on the low three percent of the growth chart. Upon reviewing records from the past pediatrician, the one the stepmother had taken him to, he had not grown and had lost 20% of his body weight in the past year. His stepmother not only used the hot sauce method for punishment, she put him on a fat free diet. Therefore, not only was he refusing to eat, when he ate, he did not get the nourishment that children need for their development, including fat (yes, that nasty word). One could only speculate what that had done to his brain development at this vulnerable age. He was now steadily increasing his food intake. I offered him scrambled eggs, pancakes, cereal and toast, bagels, juice and Ovaltine every morning for breakfast. He usually ate a hot lunch at school followed by a snack after school and then dinner. He actually began to put weight on and became more alert. However, as he put the weight on, he would grow a little, then more weight, and then grow. We could not balance the two. It took us three years before he actually grew a little and put a little weight on at the same time. He grew almost 4 inches that summer and filled his frame out nicely. He has stretch marks on his back from this rapid growth. Now his cries were, "Where's the food? I'm hungry," music to our ears. He never got heavy, because he was always very active, running, playing, and riding his bike.

Visitation eventually was resumed with his father, though it was supervised at first. Kevin began to have mixed feelings regarding the visits. He wanted to see his dad and stepbrother, but did not want to see his stepmother. As time went on, he did not always want to leave because of friends and plans he had with them. He was on a soccer team and engaged in play dates with friends. The area we had moved to had an abundance of little boys and a small wooded area behind the house. Kevin and two little boys next door began to build a fort. After school and weekends were spent gathering materials for the fort. We never spoke of any disagreements in front him and always allowed him to make the decision. At first, we tried to regain communication with his dad, for Kevin's sake. On one weekend of visitation, Kevin had a soccer game. I sent his dad a note that it was our turn to bring refreshments, so he would have to do that. My thinking was that this was a great opportunity for him to be dad and to participate in Kevin's life. Nope....cancelled visitation...did not want to do it. This began to happen regularly and it was churning in Kevin. He felt abandoned as it was, and these actions only encouraged those feelings.

As the ear infections increased, he was on antibiotic a good deal of the time. One weekend, we explained to his father that he had been sick and was on medication. We sent the medication in a bag with written note, including the pediatrician's phone number. I gave it to him on Friday when he picked up Kevin. On Saturday, Kevin broke out in hives. They did not call the pediatrician. They decided to take him to a hospital in a distant suburb where they did not inform the doctor of the existing care and treatment, making it impossible for the doctor to diagnose an allergic reaction to the medicine he was taking. We did not find out until we picked him up on Sunday night. We went to Kevin's pediatrician the next day and new medication was prescribed. He had two more allergic reactions that week, but his medical care was constant.

Kevin lost his mother before he really got to know her. He trusted in us and he lost us. He trusted in his dad and he walked away from him. What child would not have problems after this? So much loss for such a young child!

My Mom
Eulogy 5/20/03

It started out with, "I want my mommy!", and went through the stages of "Mom"and "Mother, please!", "Mom, I need help", "this is my kids' grandmother",and finally, "its okay Mom, I'm here."

Over the past week, I have had time to think about "my mom."I have thought about who she was and what she left behind after 91 years in this world. She was daughter, a wife, and a mom, grandma and great grandma. She was sister, aunt, and cousin. Though we do not have a large family, she left her mark on each of us. She was not exactly a religious person, but lived her faith quietly, attending Mass and saying the Rosary. She lived in a generation that believed that, "If I do well, if I work hard enough, if I pray enough, I will be rewarded."We all know that her life was filled with trials and losses. In preparing for today, I found the receipt for $15 paid to Mt. Carmel Cemetery in 1936, for Baby Catherine Kelly, her firstborn, the sister I never knew. She buried her husband and her first born after long battles with cancer. She buried her mother and father, her sister and her brother. Last Sunday, on

Mother's Day, we went to visit the grave of our daughter, Kathy, prior to visiting my mom in the hospital. The pain of loss and impending loss overwhelmed me, and I thought, "I can't do this."However, I remembered her quiet strength and continuing faith as she suffered through her losses, and I knew, like her, I would get the strength to carry on. She started young, caring for her younger brother and sister when she was only four, and from that point on, if someone needed help, if someone needed to be cared for, she was there, without questions, anticipating needs, giving, but not taking. It was what you should do. My Mom taught me how to live by the Ten Commandments. She taught me to, "Honor thy father and mother", as she gathered me and my sister to go with her, my dad and gram to pick up Poppy, after the inevitable call came that he needed help, he needed to be picked up, suffering from the ravages of the disease of alcoholism. I never heard her raise her voice to him. I never heard her criticize or berate him. She always said that if you do not say it, you do not have to take it back. She just picked him up and took him home to heal and be safe for awhile. He was her father and that was her duty. She took in her mother, my gram, so she would not be alone. She took in friends, relatives, and coworkers, whoever needed a place to stay or a meal to eat. If they needed money, she and my dad would give it to them. If they needed food, she would share with them what we had. I do not remember a holiday when our house was not filled with family and friends. She would work from early in the morning, days prior to the occasion, cleaning house and cooking in preparation, always worried that there would be plenty of food. She lived the commandment of Love Thy Neighbor as Thyself.

    I do not remember a vacation where some relative or friend did not join us. During the aftermath of World War II, my dad bought an old limo so the whole family could fit and go on vacation. One summer, we drove with the Schumann's to Springfield, all ten of us. Grandma Dode was with us, of course. The night we arrived, we stayed with Gram while Mom, Dad, Uncle Ken and Aunt Ethel, went out for a little while. Not like today's generation, where candy is plentiful, we bought one bag of lemon balls to share. Kenny and Patty had the idea that we could make lemonade by putting the candy in a glass of water. We spent the evening leaping from bed to bed and then to the kitchenette to see if we had lemonade yet. Grandma Dode sat in her bed, saying, "Now you kids stop that."We would say "okay"and leap across her bed and she would roar with laughter. When the adults got back, one of the beds had collapsed, Gram was laughing, and, of course, we were all hyper. But even though we got the usual, "Alright, that's enough, you kids settle down now,"I new that my mom loved that we had cousins to be with, that her mom and sister were there. There was the day that Kenny had the idea to make an elevator up to our second floor apartment. We tied the clothesline around the handles of a bushel basket we found in the yard and had Karen, because she was the youngest, get in. The three of us ran upstairs to the second floor and began to heave and ho and got Karen to the first floor, where Aunt Lucy looked out and screamed, "What are you kids doing?"Of course, in fear, we dropped the rope, and Karen, and ran. After judging there were no broken bones or permanent damage, my mom just said, "You kids shouldn't do that, somebody could have gotten hurt."We knew, without judging or berating, spankings, or time-outs, that we had made a bad choice and would not do it again. My mom knew we were just being kids and she loved that we had each other. Family meant everything to her. New Year's Eve, our house brimmed with people. Food was plentiful, as usual. Laughter rang throughout the house. At midnight, the chili that my mom and poppy had worked on all day was brought out, and everyone brought in the New Year, downing a hefty bowl of chili steaming over spaghetti. Every Easter, she made sure we had new clothes and our hair permed, to go to Church, and of course, a huge ham dinner to celebrate. She taught us the importance of Lent, of sacrificing something, the importance of confessing your sins. It was expected that you, "Honor the Sabbath day."I have tried to focus on one incident that would best describe my mom. I could not do it. Was it when she cared for Patty in her illness, never complaining, seeing to Patty's needs, taking care of her four kids and of course, keeping the house clean? Was it when she went to be with her sister in her final days? She was always caring for someone else, always putting her needs last. I wanted to be like her. I wanted to care for her needs in her final years. But, she always said, "I don't need anything." She lived the corporal works of mercy to care for the sick, feed the hungry, and bury the dead. When I was little, I was "mommy's girl." I was teased and cajoled for it. But I clung tight to the security that she gave me. Becoming an independent adult was not easy. I had such big shoes to fill to be like my mom. For a while, it did not seem possible to do, but then my sister died, and suddenly I was the only one that Mom had left. The only void I could help with was the loss of her daughter. Of course, she flew right into caring for her grandchildren, ignoring her own needs. My Mom gave up everything to be there for her grandchildren, not because she wanted anything in return, but like always, they were family, and they needed her, so she was there. Even in her declining years in the nursing home, on a unit where elderly minds were drifting in and out, she would smile, extend a hand, or just nod her assent. And others would respond to her minimal but so important support. There is many a poem written about moms and what they do for us. But today, I give testimony to my mom. In her 91 years, she never took for herself, but always gave to others, especially her family. I can only hope that if I live to be 91, that I can say I did just a little to be like her, my Mom.

After Kathy's death, my mother was deteriorating at a steady pace. Physically, she did pretty well, but her mind and memory were failing. Every day we would have these circular conversations. If you think a two year old stretches your patience, try these revolving door conversations, repeating the same thing over and over. It is easy to distract a two year old and redirect them to something else. Nevertheless, it is not as easy with an elderly person. They know in some way that their brains are not functioning well and they tend to become defensive, lashing out at those dearest to them. They do not want to admit their increasing deficiencies and who could blame them. It is an artful balance to communicate with them. Her hearing was also bad, over 50% loss in each ear. We went and got her two hearing aids, but she was devastated by them, holding her head in her hands if there was a loud noise, instead of adjusting the aids. She hated them. We returned them and I found a listening device for her to wear when she watched television. The rest of the time she would just smile and pretend that she heard. What harm was there in that? She was in her own blissful world and if she needed to hear something, I made sure she heard it. I have seen so many children of the elderly insisting their parents wear the hearing aids while the person with the hearing loss really does not care. They hear what they want and as far as they are concerned, that should be sufficient. I had her in full time adult daycare and some weekends she would go to her friend's house and the three widows would play cards, go out to dinner, and go to church. They helped each other and accepted each other for who they were....friends.

I had taken her to her friend's on Thursday night. She, as well as I, needed a respite. Her friend assured me they would look after her. On Saturday morning, I got a call from her friend that my mom had fallen and was very confused. I dashed to her house to find my mother sitting on the edge of the bed in a very soiled diaper, unsure of her surroundings and very unsteady on her feet. I estimated how I would get her down the stairs and decided there was no way, so we called for the paramedics and she was taken to the nearest hospital to be evaluated in the emergency room. She was admitted for a possible stroke. When I returned the next day, I found they had tied her to the bed because she kept on trying to crawl over the lifted bedrails and they were concerned for her safety. She barely knew who I was. I figured that God had kicked me in the butt and said, "You need to make a decision about this lady." I worked with the discharge planner and we were able to get her in a rehab facility close to our house within two days. Insurance gave me two weeks to locate a permanent facility. There was no way I could give her the care she needed at home. I had Pat, and I had Kevin and she was a full time job. She needed to be watched and occupied. She had deteriorated beyond adult daycare. I found a good nursing home near our house and had her admitted. At first she was mobile and was able to dress and feed herself. She even helped others who were less fortunate with little needs and she felt useful for this. As her mind had deteriorated, I had become the enemy. When she was in the daycare, there was a party one evening. I dropped her off at the entrance and went to park the car. When I walked in I saw this lovely social butterfly greeting everyone, smiling, laughing, and talking. The people who worked at the center were all in praise of what a wonderful lady she was. As I stood with the director of the center, I asked, "Who is that lady over there? I'd really like to meet her, because that is not the lady who lives in my house!"We both laughed because we both understood that this is the nature of Alzheimer's. However, once she was admitted to the facility, I became her friend again. I was removed from the not so envious position of caregiver. I would come and she would greet me smiling, telling everyone that I was her "baby."It was a tremendous load off my shoulders. I was still doing her laundry. My mother had this obsession of wearing the diaper, three pairs of underpants, pantyhose, and polyester slacks. How the woman did not have a constant bladder or yeast infection, I will never know. One day, Colleen and I were in to visit her and I had brought her clean laundry back and was putting it in the drawers, as well as removing the soiled things I found. As she watched me fill the bag with the soiled things, she snapped at me, "Don't take all of my socks, I don't have any."I said, "Mom, it's okay, I just put the clean ones in there."

"But you always take all my things and I can't find any,"she responded. Colleen said, "Gram, mom just put a whole bunch in the drawer for you."She doubtfully looked at me. "See, they're all in here, 12 pairs of socks."She looked at me and responded, "Well I don't know what happened, but there must have been a mother sock in there."

Holidays we tried to pick her up and bring her home. The first Thanksgiving, we picked her up early, went out to breakfast, and went to Colleen's for dinner. By 5 o'clock, my mother was getting noticeably nervous, stating that she needed to get back, they would be looking for her. She got edgy enough that Colleen and I took her back to the home. By the time we arrived, she was in increasing distress. We stopped at the nurses' station and alerted them on the way to her room. Her vital signs were all increased, temperature, blood pressure, pulse. They advised us to take her to the E.R., which we did, and spent the next four hours waiting for an answer. Eventually, they determined it was a panic attack. From that date forward, we only took her out for short visits and tried to visit her at the home on holidays, many times bringing the meal with us and joining together in a family room. She was more comfortable and that was most important. About a year after admission, she suffered bleeding ulcers and was sent to the hospital. They were concerned she might not make it because she had lost so much blood. When she returned to the home, her mind was never the same. She was in that lost world of Alzheimer's drifting between the past and the confusion of the present. She was transferred to the third floor for her safety. She remained active for a couple of years, graduating to a walker and eventually after a fall, to a wheelchair. She never had a desire to get out of it. I would frequently go to visit at dinnertime because she had stopped feeding herself. Conversation became increasingly minimal and her eyes took on a feverish, glassy look that betrayed the pain of the mind losing its grasp.

Her last birthday was her 91st. I had been coming on Monday nights to visit her and her roommate, bringing ice cream sundaes for them to enjoy while they watched Monday Night Football. That Christmas, I brought in a fiber optic Christmas tree that revolved a bright light through the green branches and draped it with pearls. Her roommate had put up several wall decorations and placed inexpensive little statues throughout the room. No one could believe how festive the little room in the nursing home became. We had some lovely memories that Christmas, especially given the surroundings. In February, her roommate who was younger and still higher functioning, died from a perferated bowel, suddenly, and without warning. She would say to me, "I don't know what I'll do when your mom goes. I'll miss her so."But it was she who died first. But the little attentions, the constant chatter of two roommates, became a loss for my mom, even though she had pretty much stopped talking. She would ask where Evelyn was and then look sadly and blankly out the window. The brightness that had been in that little room in a nursing home had dulled and the light in my mother's eyes dulled also. Two days before Mother's Day, in her 91st year, my mother was taken to the hospital gasping for breath, curled in a somewhat fetal position, her eyes staring helplessiy at the lights. Could she hear, could she see, could she understand? No one had those answers. We sat with her on Mother's Day, wiping her brow and holding her hand. There was no communication. The next day I went to see her and the doctors had ordered tests. I instructed that I did not want anything invasive done to her. I wanted her comfortable. I left the hospital that afternoon and went to the nursing home to arrange for her to come back in hospice. I returned home with the worst headache and lay down. I awoke at 5pm and started getting ready to go back to the hospital when the phone rang. My mother had passed away five minutes prior, just as I was awakening. We had all signed Power of Attorney over Healthcare when Kathy was in hospice. It was advised by the social worker as a wise thing to do. My mother had stated that she preferred to be cremated; something that had not been done previously because we were Catholic and allowing cremation was relatively new. I decided to go that route. We purchased the urn and arranged for a memorial service in two weeks, allowing my sister's children who live out of state to make plans to come. Those two weeks were so meditative for me. I wanted to write a eulogy and spent several sleepless nights working on one. What eventually developed was "My Mom." People talk about a woman's right to an abortion, about euthanasia, about not wanting to live like that if you are sick or old. Let this be my testimony. If we believed in abortion, Kevin would not be here. If we believed in euthanasia, Kathy would not have survived that last year to do what bonding she could with her son. My mom would not have lived long enough to teach me the lesson of being there for her. That is the cycle of life and I would fight forever against the right to die. If you can blink an eyelid, if you can only be present by lying there, you are giving your loved ones time to let you go, time to prepare for life without you. You cannot selfishly deny that right to your loved ones. There is no such thing as someone "wasting" away. They are a living, breathing, person who is loved and needed by their loved ones.

Kids adjust, or so they say
They forget….go on and play
Kids adjust to being ignored
Kids adjust to emotional abuse
Kids adjust to physical abuse
Kids will still play
Kids will still laugh
The play will be different
The laugh will be strained
In their eyes you will see the story told
Kids adjust, or so they say
But HOW do they adjust?

School was complicated at this time. Although we had custody, his dad still had the right to be involved in school decisions and receive reports etc. However, he had no interest in being involved. Our hands were tied as to making decisions for Kevin's education. Though Kevin was always very intelligent and scored well on intelligence testing, we did not know what damage had been done by the fat free diet. Children need fat as they grow in order for their brains to develop. Deprived of that fat, their growth may be stunted and their intelligence may suffer. At the end of fourth grade, we had Kevin's IQ tested. It came back with astonishing results. He scored in the 10th grade in cognitive math. His reading ability was over 4 years advanced of his age. His math skill levels, the redundant learning was at grade level. His writing skills were at first grade level. Was this a result of the abuse he had endured? We may never know.

 The doctors became concerned with the frequent ear infections. He should have had antibiotics and tubes earlier, but the stepmother did not believe in giving antibiotics to children because they made them hyperactive. She was so busy creating the "diarrhea"; she ignored what was happening to Kevin. On the last day of 1st grade, Kevin was in the hospital to have surgery to remove a tumor that was growing in his left ear. It was formed from scar tissue from the numerous ear infections. Fifteen years ago, this was a common occurrence, but when they started giving antibiotics and inserting the tubes, this type of growth became minimal in numbers. By the time it was found in Kevin, it had destroyed 95% of the conductive hearing bones in his left ear, leaving him with at least a 70% loss of hearing in that ear. Second grade became demanding because he was easily distracted and began to gain a reputation of "not listening." We had to wait for full healing to occur before we would know the total loss of hearing. During this time, he was treated like any other child, and "not listening" branded him a "bad boy." He spoke loudly and was easily distracted, characteristics that we found later, were due to his hearing loss. After the hearing loss was confirmed, they assigned a hearing itinerant teacher to him and he got a hearing aid, as well as an FM unit. An FM unit is a teaching device for the hearing impaired where the teacher wears a speaker unit around her neck and the child wears a receiver, like a hearing aid. The teacher's voice goes directly to the child, in an attempt to override peripheral noises in the room like other children's voices, doors opening and closing, papers crunching, and coughing. The teacher was reluctant, stating it caused a disruption in her class. She refused to place Kevin in the seating the itinerant recommended, which was meant to diminish distractions for Kevin. I received a note one day that Kevin had been in the washroom for over 30 minutes. I immediately questioned her as to who was in charge that my six year old was out of supervision for that amount of time. Kevin told me he had left with the FM unit in his ear and could hear everything the teacher said while he was in the washroom. As he began to meet with the itinerant, he started to learn listening skills, and lip reading. He learned to turn his "good" ear to the speaker. He also starting to see an occupational therapist to deal with his writing skills. This therapy consisted of him learning how to hold a pencil properly and when he knew that, he was no longer eligible for therapy. He was also to receive social services. He saw the social worker one to two times per week. She said that she and the principal were both convinced that he suffered from ADHD and needed medication. Medication would quiet him down and reduce his disruptions in class. Of course, this started the war that would continue through Kevin's school years. The labels were attached. He was a "spoiled brat who did not listen, and was disruptive in class." We were the aged grandparents who did not know education today and were spoiling him. Third grade brought Kevin a teacher who was a gift from above. Her patience and one-on-one with each of her students, made third grade the best year he had. The first day he was in her class, Kevin jumped in the car and said, "I've got the nicest teacher, and you know what? She doesn't know HOW to scream. That's what she told us!" When occupational therapy stopped, we requested that the social worker visits stop also. Being pulled out of class constantly was wearing on his ability to perform in class. We asked that he only be taken out to meet with the hearing itinerant. We kept Kevin involved in activities. He played soccer, took marshal arts, and went to religious education. He continued to make friends easily and was a happy kid. He did continue to have problems with school. Every year, he would start out with teachers pulling their hair out. It was as if he was testing them to see if he were bad enough, would they too reject him as so many others had. By the end of January each year, in the teacher's eyes, Kevin suddenly became a great kid and they could not understand the change. It was not Kevin that changed, it was their perspective.

Fourth grade brought another disaster in teachers. He was assigned to a teacher who had been in the business world and was returning to her "calling" to teach. I doubt that she exhibited much business sense and certainly lacked in teaching skills. She was disorganized, constantly moved the children's desks around, (when Kevin was out with chickenpox, he came back and sat in his desk when another boy approached him and said, "Hey, that's my desk now." Kevin had no idea where his desk was!) She hysterically screamed at the children while they were getting ready to leave at the end of the day. Now, you might say that this can be typical in a classroom. However, when you are hearing impaired, it is a huge problem. Kevin's hearing aide exacerbated noises, like screaming, talking, doors slamming, and chairs being pushed in and out. It was a literally painful time of day for him. This was also when she would scream out the homework assignments, which Kevin usually missed. She refused to keep Kevin seated per the recommendations and Kevin began to lose, little by little, until he just tried to get out of her class. If he talked and was disruptive, he was put in the hall. He would leave for extended visits to the bathroom, plead that he was ill and needed to go to the nurse's office, or just sneak out and roam the hall until he was caught. At the parent/teacher conference, and the IEP meetings I asked if they did not see a pattern and that perhaps, they were not meeting Kevin's needs. Of course, they refused to consider this....Kevin was purposefully bad and we were senile.

Fifth grade brought a change in Kevin's life. He went to a school that was for fifth and sixth graders only. It was a different school and kids from other grade schools in the district were added to the mixture. At the IEP meeting at the end of school year for 4th grade, we approached the meeting with a letter stating that we were not happy with Kevin's progress. We felt that perhaps we needed to look at Kevin having additional problems beyond the hearing loss. We were astonished at the great discrepancy between reading at 8th grade level and writing at 1st grade level. They huffed, they puffed, and they tried to blow us down. What did we want? Kevin needed to be responsible. As we had expressed so many times before, we asked that they please understand that Kevin had been through a lot in his younger years and was still battling many issues. "He should be over that by now....he just doesn't want to do the work." We responded that though it was in the past, and he was growing well within our care, the baggage was there and needed to be dealt with. We sought legal assistance to help. Just prior to school starting, we met with the special education director, teachers and principal. They asked what we wanted. "We want Kevin to receive the help he needs to learn." We offered that the broad discrepancy in reading vs. handwriting might be helped by Kevin having a laptop computer. They huffed, they puffed, and they got people to test Kevin. Kevin could write, albeit with problems, so he did not need the computer. They placed him in an REI classroom, (Regular Education Initiative). We found out later, the class consisted of 27 students, 23 of which were learning disabled and unable to function in the regular classroom, 2 behavior disordered children, one of which acted out loudly and grossly, and Kevin. They sat Kevin next to the student who frequently was loud and abusive and acted out on a regular basis. This was a great distraction to Kevin with his hearing problem, but he construed the boy to be his "friend." This only exacerbated the judgments already in place. He had now made his choice to be with a boy who of course, taught him behaviors we did not seek for him to learn. The LD teacher was assigned half time to this classroom and was supposed to help Kevin with his writing skills and help him to develop the skill of maintaining an assignment book, a skill that had totally evaded Kevin, even with my organizational bag of tricks to help him. The first day of school, she wrote, "Kevin, I wrote your assignments today, but from now on it's your job"....end of responsibility for teacher...... Things deteriorated. In May of that year, Kevin began to complain of a piercing pain in his left ear. We saw his ear doctor who said he thought it might be pain from TMJ. and referred us to the University of Illinois for an evaluation. Diagnosis was negative for TMJ. The piercing pain decreased but dizzy spells began to increase. We were referred to a neurologist for evaluation at Highland Park Hospital. Kevin endured his first MRI in a noisy, clanging machine. He was wonderful! They praised his cooperation in the test. Diagnosis unknown. We had repeated follow-ups with this doctor for a few months with no relief. He prescribed an anti-seizure medication, which should stop the dizzy spells. Instead, Kevin had the opposite reaction. They increased and vertigo set in. He passed out. We were walking down the hall of an office building when he stopped and began to slide to the floor, saying it was like there was a "gray curtain" in front of his eyes. We went Christmas shopping and he began the same thing in the middle of a large department store. I eased him to a short display and Pat got out of his wheelchair so I could drop Kevin into it. We walked slowly out to the mall and after about 20 minutes, he sat up and said, "Oh, I guess I fell asleep." We believe he passed out. He was holding his hand over his eyes, shielding his eyes from the light and we could not tell whether he was "asleep" or had passed out. Our worries increased. We went back to his ear doctor and expressed our frustration in not finding an answer. Dizzy spells led to nausea. Kevin ran from the classroom up to 12 times per day to vomit. Not once, did a teacher go, or send a student to check on him. When the dizziness and nausea went away, he returned to the classroom. We took him out of marshal arts because he was unable to complete a class without the dizziness and nausea disrupting him. He remained in his dance company where teachers noted he would turn gray and slip to the floor when these "attacks"hit. The ear doctor referred us to Children's Memorial Hospital Hearing Clinic where the doctor suspected a fistula, which was a small hole in his eardrum that was allowing fluids in the inner ear to mix, causing the dizziness. She referred us to a specialist at Northwestern University who specialized in dizziness and vertigo. He normally did not treat children, but agreed to test him. He confirmed a strong possibility that there was indeed a fistula. During this four-month period from September to December, the school battle raged. Kevin was shown no mercy. The assistant principal constantly harassed him, reprimanding him for every little thing, following him in the hall, in the lunchroom, on the playground. She approached me one day and said, "You know I believe Kevin is faking this and the teachers agree with me….he's just trying to get out of doing his work."One afternoon, we were at the lawyer's office trying to find out what we could do to protect Kevin. On coming in from lunch recess, another boy picked up a piece of concrete and slammed it on Kevin's instep, causing a great deal of pain. He was taken to the nurse's office where he laid for two and a half hours with a damp wet paper towel on his foot. When I arrived to pick him up, he did not come out to the car. I went into the school where I found him still lying in the nurse's office, alone. The nurse had gone home. I asked why they did not call my daughter who lived three blocks from the school. They stated they did not have that information and there were no emergency numbers on his sheet in their book. I asked why they did not call the paramedics if they could not reach anyone. "Why should we call the paramedics? They don't come for that type of thing, he's alright."I was fuming, knowing the number of small bones in his foot that could have broken and the fact that they had callously left him lie there all afternoon. The assistant principal pointed out the sheet in the book and I was more furious. This was not the sheet I had filled out that year. It was the sheet I had filled out for first grade. Miraculously, they found the proper sheet the next day. I took Kevin home, getting him to the car on my own, because not one person offered to help. I iced and wrapped his foot and watched it for 24 hours. Signs of a break should have shown up by that time. It was however, a very painful injury as anyone who has ever had a hard object dropped on the top of their foot, especially a slab of concrete. This was October. Every time we kept Kevin out of school to go to yet another doctor or hospital, the assistant principal laid in wait for his return. In looking back at the records, she gave him 36 detentions that year, following him, harassing him, calling him names, accusing him of every wrong doing from whispering to getting into a fight with a boy who was constantly teasing him about his hearing aid, calling him an "old man" because he needed a hearing aid. The fights were always his fault, as far as she was concerned. By early December, when his ear doctor decided to do surgery, I realized it was dangerous for Kevin to be in that school. After commenting frequently about no one checking on him when he ran to the bathroom, his teacher followed him ONCE! He told me he went into the stall where Kevin had been "making vomiting noises" and saw nothing in the toilet bowl, so therefore assumed Kevin was "faking." I asked him if he ever hear of the dry heaves. Kevin's appetite was down considerably because of all of this and he probably had nothing in his stomach to vomit. I gave a letter to the principal, stating I was concerned for my son's safety in the school, and would be keeping him home until the surgery, and asked for a tutor to work with him at home. They waited two weeks to send a tutor and she was barely able to give him two weeks tutoring. She thought he was the greatest kid, praised his work, and praised us for the job we were doing with him. Kevin had surgery to implant a new prosthesis bone for conductive hearing and a "patch" to close the expected fistula. The day after the surgery, he was a different kid. He did not have any more dizzy spells from that day forward. He returned to school about two weeks after the surgery and I met with the principal, demanding a classroom change and insisted that he pull his assistant principal off Kevin's back. I met her face to face in the hall and literally told her to "back off" on harassing Kevin. She acted horrified that I would say such a thing. We then were constantly attacked by the principal and his new teacher, repeatedly blaming Kevin, and/or us for his problems, insisting the fault should be on us, not them. I myself was sick to my stomach, with the calloused behavior of these so-called "professionals." By the end of the year, we made the decision to file for a Due Process Hearing. We could not afford a lawyer so we approached the process on our own. We made a laughing stock of ourselves. We were ill prepared and the hearing officer shared no mercy in expressing his exasperation with our inability to define the process and make the proper statements. As we approached the fall, it was clear there would be no agreement so we asked for a hearing. We arrived at the hearing, Pat and I on one side of the table, the hearing officer, and court reporter at the end, and the Special Education Director, her assistant, and three lawyers for the district, who specialized in these hearings. As in the old gunslinger movies, we were outnumbered. Custer's Last Stand was to play out here. I confidently presented the case the best I could. When the teachers were up, they stated they thought Kevin was faking because he did not want to do the work. I asked them why they did not call his doctor if they felt so strongly that he was faking. I asked them if they felt the doctor performed unnecessary surgery, pointing out that it was their obligation as licensed professionals to protect the child if they felt so strongly about it. They lied under oath and did not blink an eye. Their attorneys, paid for by the school district, constantly criticized my questioning. It was truly a kangaroo court, one I found on research, is played out on a regular basis with parents fighting for their children against hired legal guns, who make big money specializing in fighting the parents and saving the school district. The decision at the end was that the school district had offered Kevin a free and appropriate education and he had chosen not to accept it. If he could add two and two and read a few words, they had done their job and we had no right to challenge them. Amen.

During this time in Kevin's life, his distrust of teachers, and adults in general, increased. I could only remain his port in the storm, but even that relationship was on shaky ground because of the necessity to discipline him for not doing work or getting into fights. I was always haunted by my feelings that he really did not want to be this way, but he did not know how to be otherwise. We trusted the so-called professionals in teachers, social workers, principals, and administrators. We believed that they were licensed because of the increased education in knowing to teach children. We were grossly wrong. We found out that the Director of Special Education was a Special Ed teacher, period. No special knowledge of how to direct the department. Her chosen assistant, the school psychologist, whom we trusted was a doctor of psychology, turned out to have an advanced education in administration, not psychology. I was appalled to find out in my research that in our state school psychologists do not have to have a doctor of psychology. If someone could explain the rational of this, I would greatly appreciate it! These people are advising parents of children on medication for seizures, ADD, ADHD, and numerous other conditions. Legally, they are supposed to refer parents to their doctors. This one took it upon herself to tell parents to increase medications because their children were too much of a problem for their teachers. How could anyone with an administration degree know whether children were "at risk,"ADD, ADHD, or anything else? However, this was the power she had, and she used it. I began to speak with other parents and was left speechless with what I heard. Children locked in conference rooms until they finished their work, placed in the hall for entire days, children berated and told they were "bad,"and there was "no hope"for them. One parent told me her 13-year-old son was locked in the conference room to complete his work after numerous time periods spent sitting in the hall. The only way she found out was when they called to inform her he was injured. He became so frustrated, being locked in the room, and he urinated in the wall outlet and received a significant electric shock. Now, you may say this child was a problem, but the bottom line is that both teachers and administrators are supposed to be competent enough to handle these situations. If a parent were found to be locking their child in a room, family services would be called, the children removed, and the parent jailed. Yet, teachers and administrators get away with this. I believe that a parent should be able to trust that the teachers of their children, and the administrators of the schools, should know, and understand, what it takes to teach children, especially children of today's complicated world. Our educational system is no different than the proverbial little red schoolhouse of years past. Children fall into groups and are labeled as such. Individualism is too much trouble for teachers. Yet, teaching one on one is exactly what children need, especially with problems facing them today, such as divorce, abuse, loss, and generally living in a far more competitive world than any adult has had too. We hear all the time about what teachers have to put up with in unreasonable children, and inadequate parents. I believe it is time to stand up for the children and their parents who care, to be heard. It is time for change. The repetitive "if we only had more money" is worn out. It has been proven that even when a great deal of money was pumped into the schools, results did not increase. In fact, it usually resulted in lower test scores, more problems within the schools and generally more of a hindrance than a help. In any school district in America, a review of the budget will show administrative salaries that compare with top-level executives in the business world. Yet, if the executive does not show improved performance, he is fired. Tenured teachers, in many districts, make more than full time businesspersons do, many times in the six-figure range. Businesspersons work 50/60 hours per week and are judged by their performance. If it is not there, they either are fired or get a reduction in pay. Tenured teachers have 12 weeks paid vacation off per year. They cannot be reprimanded unless they break the law, and they are guaranteed this salary until they decide to retire. For those of you who get upset with me on this subject, I suggest you start investigating your own school district. Teachers and administrators salaries are easily accessible. In our state our past governor is on trial for taking bribes, like vacations, cars, dinners, favors. School administrators drive very expensive luxury cars, and take extensive summer vacations in Europe. Teachers drive up in their Mercedes Benz and take cruises. Yet, the administrator can be too busy to speak to a parent without an appointment, or refer them to someone else. A teacher can complain that she just "doesn't have the time to handle your child." Is this true in all school districts? Of course not, but the same mentality seems to rule education today, and it must be changed. Just look at the statistics of how many parents are now home schooling, after years of frustration with school districts. The only reason I spend the time on this subject is that I know that Kevin's life would be different if he had teachers who would invest the time into finding the way to teach him. The destruction for children like Kevin is that teachers build a characteristic of poor self-confidence and lack of trust into these kids, because they do not know, or do not want to spend the time to learn how to help them. We considered the possibility of home schooling, but not everyone can qualify and you also take away the important socialization of being in a school environment. We could not take Kevin and keep him home alone. Our quest has been to find a school district we could trust with teachers and administrators who cared enough to work with each child and his/her needs.

When we moved, we thought we had found that. The schools were "Blue Ribbon" and we were encouraged that there was an answer here. Unfortunately, we did not move until he was in 7th grade, many bad habits had been formed, and the lack of study skills was serious. We were honest with the new school and offered to work with them to find the answer for Kevin. That was not enough. While they did not lock the children in a room, a disciplinary practice was to put children in a "time out" room where they needed to sit in a lowly lit room and do nothing. If work was allowed, the student was on his own with minimal or no help. This is how the student spends the day as punishment for whatever infraction they were guilty of. No learning, no teaching, just sitting and do not dare fall asleep from boredom or you will be punished for that too. How do I know this? I complained enough that they allowed me to come one day and stay in the room with Kevin and three other boys. There was an employee, not a teacher, who sat in the room and read a magazine. A teacher came in later, but only after she saw me, did she attempt to offer help. Now mind you, offering help to kids who have been kicked out of class because they have not done work is mindless. These kids are already in learning trouble and need a great deal of individualized help, encouragement, and structure.

ABC, 123, 2+2 and 4+4
Happy, happy shall I be,
When I have learned….
I meant to do my work, I really did
3x6, 24 divided by 8
Three paragraph essays, 5 paragraph essays
Spelling, history, computers….I really do want to learn
But….something goes wrong and teacher gets mad
She thinks I'm being disrespectful….now I'm in trouble
I didn't mean it…really I didn't
Marshall Arts, band, science club and chorus
They sound like fun but……
I can't….I didn't finish my work….again
I really didn't mean to forget my homework…
I really didn't mean to lie….I was in deep trouble
So I said the first thing that came to my mind.
So, here I am now, again in detention.
I wonder what my classmates are learning today.
I wish I could learn too….I really do.

Kevin was reluctantly graduated from 8th grade. In the national testing at the end of 8th grade, Kevin was rated in 93% nationwide. Yet, he was failing in his school. Nevertheless they agreed to allow him to graduate. It was a joyous moment for us, but a very cold, unwelcome greeting from the school staff when we arrived for the ceremony. It had been a battle to get them to allow Kevin extra time to finish his work. He was worn out from the migraines that were coming almost daily. He was attempting to complete the work from teachers. No deals were to be made. He completed the work or he would not graduate. Mind you, I was not looking for dispensation for him. The math teacher who was of course, tenured, and made almost $90,000 a year, was the major player in all of this. She was firm. Complete the assignments to her liking, or she would not pass him. The fact that both his neurologist and pediatrician had written letters to the school, asking for some leniency because of the headaches, did not factor in. They were ignored. The entire staff was oblivious to what was going on with Kevin. He did not fit the mold, so therefore there was no plan for him. Is he unique in his needs? Absolutely not! Many kids out there are hurting. Divorce, death, drugs, mental illness, lack of parenting skills, are a few of the reasons that so many kids are in similar predicaments. None of them fit the molds. It is always assumed by teachers and a good deal of school psychologists and social workers that the child is to blame because they will not do the work, or they misbehave, or they're lazy, or the parents are not supportive. Never, ever, is it the fault of the educators. Yet, if you think about it, they have your children for at least six hours a day. Six hours to a working parent would be considered a blessing! Talk about quality time! Teachers today have the ability to make very nice salaries, from $80,000 to $200,000 per year, depending on the district. While they do not start at that level, they have the ability to become tenured and earn the higher salaries within 10 years of their start. What other job offers this kind of security? Teachers are busy planning their spring break cruises, their summer vacations to Europe. They have unions that build in time for them to take off for their needs and protect their job security, and get them the highest salaries. Who suffers if they do not get what they want? The children. I grew up in an era where we respected teachers. I went to a parochial school where the nuns were next to God. Our parents always supported the teachers. Why? Because the majority of my parent's generation were lesser educated and parented by the seat of their pants. They were taught to respect teachers, police officers, doctors, priests, and ministers. This group of people could no wrong. They were sainted. They were not to be questioned. Their word was God's word. You did not argue with it. Although they had this extreme high level of respect, society did not see fit to compensate their needs monetarily. However, that was then, and this is now. You ask for a second opinion from your doctor. You tell your priest if you disagree with his preachings, and then go church shopping if you are not happy with his answer. But you are not allowed to question your child's teacher, and if you do, you and your child are labeled, and life will not be easy for either of you. Education has formed its own little society with its own rules and judgments. Teachers and administrators openly share their opinions of a child and/or the parent and their judgment will go with that child the rest of their life. Should this not be grounds for a second opinion? I am not giving education a bad rap. I am not retaliating in anger over what happened to our son. I am stating that after raising not one, but two families, I feel qualified to have a significant opinion on education. We are 100 years past the little red schoolhouse and yet we are looking at education in the same way.

Let me close the chapter on Kevin's education with one last story. As predicted, high school was overwhelming for Kevin. He was not prepared and it ate him up. By the end of his first semester as a freshman, he was referred to an alternative high school, where he attended for three hours per day and worked on a computer to complete his work. He did wonderfully. By the end of his first year, we requested that he be placed back in the regular high school, as we had been told he would be. His counselor quickly set us straight that he was not welcome to come back and that he must finish one year at the alternative school. I pushed hard, reiterating their promise that if he did well for the semester he would be welcomed back in the fall. I lost that argument, but I fought again for him to be retested and a plan be implemented that would meet his needs at school. I won that. After complete testing, we had an IEP meeting with 14 people present. Kevin was amazed at the people involved in planning for his education. For the first time, there were positives. No one blamed Kevin, or us. The psychologist stated he was a normal kid and a very nice one at that. The hearing itinerant had a plan to work with each of his teachers to help them understand his problems in a classroom environment with his type of hearing loss. The assistant principal offered to oversee the plan. We left the IEP meeting with a feeling of support, for the first time in nine years. The only negative was his counselor who kept stating, "He can't do that." We requested a new counselor. So far, he has been too busy to meet with us. However, the testing, the therapies, are opening doors into insight for us and most especially for Kevin. If we can identify the problem, we can find a solution. We have also been participating in therapy at a local community service group that specializes in helping kids, mostly teens. It has changed our lives. For the first time, we have support for Kevin, and for us as parents. For the first time, therapist and teachers are acknowledging Kevin's past and understanding the baggage he has to deal with.

Yesterday, we made a giant leap. Kevin has cut his English and his Math classes, but proceeded to go to the last three periods of classes. Why? We had worked all weekend on a speech to be given in his first period English class and he had a test to make up in Math. Did he accomplish this? No. Where did he go? He wandered around the school halls. Why? He was scared and did not know what to do. When I came to school to pick him up, we had a meeting with his the assistant principal and we all expressed frustration with Kevin's actions. Why would he cut a class that he had spent all weekend working hard in preparation for? Later that day, as I spoke with Pat, both us again expressing frustration, my memory clicked in. We remembered when they called us in kindergarten and said he asked to go the washroom and was found wandering around the school. In first grade they expressed concern because he left the classroom and was found wandering the school. There were incidents in 2nd grade, 3rd grade, and 4th grade, where he was found wandering the halls, or staying in the bathroom for 30 minutes. The teacher repeatedly put him in the hall because he was "not listening."(The child with the hearing impairment!) In Jr. High he was again caught wandering the halls during class and eventually was put into a time-out room where he was secluded from the rest of the school in a darkened, quiet, room. He was supposed to get one-on-one help from a teacher. This did not always occur and he frequently told us he slept while in time-out. This was supposed to teach him? When his stepmother locked him in his bedroom, he told us how he and his stepbrother climbed out of the bedroom window and roamed the neighborhood looking for kids to play with. He always complained of the noisy environment in the classroom.

The pieces all suddenly fell together. He had developed a skill to deal with things that were overwhelming. Time-out rooms were a recluse for him. Quiet hallways, where traffic was almost nonexistent because everyone was in class, were a recluse for him. Teachers had enabled him to use this as a recluse. We talked with Kevin last night about these experiences and helped him to see the pattern and explained to him that he now has a choice and if he so chooses, he can break this pattern. It will not be easy and we have spoken to his administrator and his therapist to help them to help Kevin. What will the remainder of his educational years bring? I do not know. The fight is his now. He finally has a lot of support, but needs to develop the skills to use that support. The one thing we know for sure. It is not his fault. It is the fault of the adults in his life who have failed him. Now, we must be there to help him overcome the damages done by those adults. I have faith that Kevin will do it. I have faith that he will be successful in whatever he does. I know it will be hard. I know that overcoming any bad habit is uphill all the way.

The other factor is that Kevin continues to have serious health issues. His hearing loss has been dealt with, though he needs to be monitored. At ten, he was diagnosed with Spina Bifida Occulta, the least serious form of the condition. However, he suffers from chronic back pain that has an effect on the way he lives his life. Again, we finally have been referred to a doctor who specializes in this condition. However, he has found that this condition is the least of Kevin's worries. When we told him of chronic insomnia and migraine headaches he decided to look deeper to find out why Kevin was suffering these things at such a young age. He ordered a sleep study, which identified restless leg syndrome. The doctor decided that with the health history of his biological father, who was diagnosed with a dystonia syndrome and now the diagnosis of restless leg in Kevin, that it would be a good idea to do some tests. Last month we were faced with the results of these tests, which led the doctor to consider that Kevin has inherited a rare genetic disease, which can lead to death before age 30, if not properly diagnosed and treated. He has had several tests so far and only one continues to be suspicious, meaning the diagnosis cannot be confirmed. He will be watched for symptoms. The disease is caused by the individual's low level of the enzyme that processes copper in the blood. If the copper is not processed through the body, it accumulates in the liver and the brain, and eventually destroys them. We will win this one because we know what the problem is and can get treatment. He will survive.

Just imagine being 16 years old and receiving that kind of news! After the doctor told us, he looked at Kevin and said, "You're not saying anything. If I had just been told what I have told you, I would be screaming my head off." Kevin had no response. He was stunned. Still, very heavy stuff for a young kid who has already been through so much. The doctor feels that his father's condition is relative to him having the same disease.

We have been going to Physical Therapy for several weeks now. They have found that Kevin's lungs have never fully developed to their potential. It is usual for a preemie to have lung problems when they are born. We all assume that the lungs will develop with everything else, as normal, unless a serious condition is diagnosed. However, he has just never learned to use his lungs to capacity because he did not know he had that control. However, the shallow breathing has effects on the rest of his body and unless therapy is done to reverse the damage, it will get worse. His right hip does not work as well and if he is not rotated, his right leg is shorter than the left. So every week, the adjustment must be made to get his legs at the same length. No wonder he has had chronic back pain! Yesterday, we saw an occupational therapist that specializes in certain Asian therapies. I can only relate this in nonprofessional terms as my intent is not to write a book on medical treatments and therapies. The bottom line is that at the end of the evaluation, she reiterated what the physical therapist had said, that his spine is rigid from his neck down. The occupational therapist states it is a result of his Spina Bifida Occulta. His brain has sensed a "hole" in the lumbar region. Since it cannot fill that "hole," it is sending the message through his nervous system not to move, freezing movement to avoid pain.

She also said that the abuse he received in eating has forced him to feel he does not deserve to eat. He was conditioned for this. So when he eats, he may have indigestion, poor appetite, or binge when he gets hungry. Now you may say this is all hocus pocus, but it fits! As we spoke with his therapist later that day, we unfolded again stories of how he ate and the problems we have had, and again with no answers. Now we have an answer. Now Kevin has an answer. Now Kevin can give himself permission to eat and enjoy it, and know that he will not be punished with hot sauce if he does not want to eat something.

HAS ANYONE SEEN MY DAISY?

"Kids adjust"……….yeah they sure do. However, why must they adjust to abuse instead of nurturing? Why must they adjust to anger instead of love? Why can't their needs be put first? The laws have parent rights, father's rights, mother's rights….what about children's rights. I once spoke with a teenager who was in a psychiatric hospital. He was a nice kid, but he had gotten into trouble at home and at school. He was full of remorse and wanted to make things better. He was being tested to look for psychological damage. His father was too busy with his new life to come to the hospital. His mother had a job and a new boyfriend and blamed him for causing her so many problems. He was 15 years old! We cannot possibly expect kids who are emotionally and physically abused to learn the skill of increasing responsibility. They are in the defense mode, in their own homes! They are trying to survive. They are daily subjected to the poor parenting skills of so many adults, from all socioeconomic backgrounds. Being poor does not make you a bad parent. Being wealthy does not make you a good parent. If you are more concerned with getting your nails done, going to the gym, shopping for your new wardrobe, or on the phone complaining about your kids, you are not parenting! Kids needs attention, lots of it. You cannot look at them when they go to high school and say, "What's wrong with you?" What is wrong is that you have not been around for them and they have turned to survival mode and probably feel resentment towards you for putting them in that position. In twenty years, it will not matter what type of house of you lived in, or what kind of clothes you wore. All they will remember is if you were there for them. If you think because you have a college degree and a good job, you are going to make a good parent, think again! Everyone falls in love with the idea of getting pregnant and starting a family. Families who cannot get pregnant are spending huge amounts of money on adoptions from foreign countries or invitro fertilization to fulfill the dream of family. No matter where they come from, they will need you 24/7 and that is the sacrifice you will make for being a parent. Are you ready? Your reward will be seeing that child grow up to be successful in their family life. A lot is said about extended families. Only some cultures retain that today. Elderly people get in the way. Grandparents should mind their own business. Young parents respect the books they read more than listening to their parents. Yet, an extended family relationship is what children need. Yes, you will have disagreements and you will not always get the other side to think like you, but that is life! Deal with it! Your kids will benefit from it, I guarantee. Why are so many grandparents today raising their grandchildren? Many times it is because of illness or death, but more likely it's because of drugs, alcohol and mental illness. Grandparents today were taught to be responsible for family, to defend the rights of children and the elderly. If we do not go back to this, our society will continue to decline. Today's young parents have power. As a whole, they have high levels of education and careers with six figure incomes. They live in homes with bathrooms so large, I would be intimidated to be naked in them. They drive cars that cost as much as our dream house did. They take luxurious vacations. They have "quality time"for mom, for dad, and lastly for kids. They have the highest level of disposable income in our history. They think nothing of spending $300 on a concert ticket and pay babysitters $100 so they can leave the kids home and enjoy their concert. The bottom line is that if they do not have the parenting skills, none of this will mean anything. Everything will be a disappointment.

This generation also has better than half of their population divorced, with kids. So now kids must adapt to step dad, step mom, and spend one week with one parent and the other week with the other parent. What happened to being a child, coming home to mom and dad and having a family dinner? I know that times are different, but this is the kind of thing that kids need if they are to grow. They need adults to be adults. It is up to the parents to set the structure for the teen. There must be a moat around the castle of your home and there must be plans to fight off the intruders, even the ones from with the walls, like TV and the Internet. We must remove our heads from the sand and realize what is attacking teens today. You might say, "Well, they're 16 years old!"Maybe, but they are not adults and do not have what they need to survive many situations. Yet, our laws are prosecuting teens as adults. It is a mixed message we send to them.

HAS ANYONE SEEN MY DAISY?

When I was 16, it was "sweet sixteen." When my children's generation was 16, it was the "cool years." Teens strove to be accepted as adults. But today, when statistics show a huge percentage of children having sex by the time they are nine years old, when 13, 14, 15, and 16 year olds are getting their grandparents guns and shooting up schools, only a fool would comment, "What's wrong with kids today?" What is wrong? The adults in their lives are not doing their job! It is parents who are worried about what they get out of life, it is teachers who say, "That's not my job," it is police officer with zero tolerance, who say, "No kid will get away with that on my beat." Perhaps, it is just a thought, we could start looking at those teens, see through the toughness, and realize that underneath are scared, defensive children who have been let down and have nowhere to go for support, unless they fit the scenario painted by adults in their lives. Teens are supposed to be able to experiment, but with parental support and structure. What happened to this? The next time you approach your teen and they say the usual, "Who cares," try responding, "I care and I'm not going to let you hurt yourself. I'm going to stand by you, even if you don't think you want me, because I love you, and I care." Whether it is the first, second, or fifth time you have this exchange, the teen will come to know that you are not going to give up on them, and that yes, you do care. You might need to accept the bizarre styles, the body piercing, the fowl language, but as you gain their trust, they will seek better ways. Adolescent Psychology, simple and basic. Try it.

We have learned so much this year. The answers are coming, though not necessarily the answers we want. The challenges are immense and the job is far from done. Neurologists, social workers, physical therapists, occupational therapists, are working together. Kevin no longer has to feel that it is his fault. It is not. The damages were done many years ago in his early youth. The abuse, neglect, and so many losses did leave their mark. The scars will never totally go away. But acknowledging them and getting a plan and support system going will make the difference. It's not Kevin's fault, no more than it is any child's fault that they lose a parent, suffer abuse or neglect, and have their lives altered before they could get through the playful period. Yes, it is hard work, but we must persist in our efforts to give these kids a break. "It will not matter what kind of house they lived in,"or the wealth of their belongings. It will matter how much love and understanding they received. That will make the difference. That will give them a fair chance at a normal adulthood. Today, a therapist explained that no matter how much we may want Kevin to be at a certain place, he is not. Expecting him to perform at that place may not be realistic. He has to get over the negative feelings left by the abuse and neglect in order to get to the place where he can move forward. It is a long journey, one for body and soul, one that is as precarious as mountain climbing, but one that must be taken. When he reaches the top of the pinnacle, then he will be ready, not before.

My heart is full of things to say, to share what I have learned. However, I feel it time to end this book. It is not the end of the story. It is the beginning of Kevin's life. He will write the rest of the story. He needs us there for a few more years, but decisions will be more his than ours. We will continue to provide the structure and support even when he thinks he does not want it. We will continue to reinforce his responsibilities for decisions he makes. We will continue to be there for him when he makes a mistake. We will not berate him for those mistakes, but will talk about them, and help him learn from his mistakes. I am hopeful that he will turn into a responsible adult and then he will write the rest of the story. You cannot plan what your child will be. You can teach them, you can discipline them, you can love them. You can let them know you love them and will support them, through everything.

To Kevin, with love,
Daisy

Father's Day, June 2000

Thank you Father for….
Keeping me updated on the news
Walking the dog
Loving me
Raising me
Teaching me how to defend myself
Making chili
Being there.

Love to you,
Kevin

6/17/05

Summer Workshop in New York

Hey, what's going on? I'm having a great time here. But I'm very busy. We've had a guest speaker every day, and great classes with them. I'm taking some awesome classes like Fosse and a course on writing. I'm out of time, but I will write again!

Love,
Kevin

My Mother's Day Card from Kevin
5/13/07

Only Certain People See the Good in Every Day
By Emily Matthews

Only certain people can see the gifts that each day brings
and wonder at the miracles in ordinary things, when thoughts and words are hasty and perhaps misunderstood,
They look beyond the obvious to find what's true and good,
Their vision of life's promise and the hope they share each day, make a difference in the hearts of those they touch along life's way.

Because you look for the good in life, you're quick to share a smile; you see the best in others, (though that's always been your style)

Love, Kevin

Also available from PublishAmerica
A CAN OF MAGIC SMILES
by Elizabeth E. Rogers

Grandma keeps a can of magic smiles in her cupboard. Her grandchildren think the can is empty, until Grandma puts a smile on her granddaughter's face from the can. Grandma time is very special time to children.

Paperback, 28 pages
8.5" x 8.5"
ISBN 1-4241-8671-4

About the author:

Elizabeth E. Rogers has lived in Central California most of her life. Having been born in Arkansas, she has a strong Southern influence. Learning the art of story telling from her grandmother, Emma, she draws wisdom and strength from the traditions she was taught. She says her grandmother was the perfect role model. Elizabeth has been writing short stories since she was a child. The children in *A Can Of Magic Smiles* are her own grandchildren. Elizabeth is the mother of five children: three daughters and two sons. Elizabeth's daughter is the one who urged her to write some of her stories. Two of her daughters have myotonic muscular dystrophy. She is raising one of her grandsons, who also has muscular dystrophy. Now single after a 23 year marriage and just starting her career as an author of children's books, *A Can Of Magic Smiles* is her first published work. Drawing inspiration from everyday life and her family, Elizabeth plans to continue writing children's books. She says writing allows her to be creative and stay at home to care for her children.

Available to all bookstores nationwide.
www.publishamerica.com

Also available from PublishAmerica

COME AND MEET BACI
by Diana Granata

A story told by Baci, an Italian Greyhound, sharing his ancestry, personality, characteristics and traits of being a royal dog. Baci believes that to love where you come from and enjoy your individuality is what makes each of us special.

Paperback, 39 pages
8.5" x 8.5"
ISBN 1-60474-463-4

About the author:

A 30-year resident of Connecticut, I still retain a fondness for my birthplace and true "home" — Italy. Choosing Baci, my Italian Greyhound, brings me closer to my roots on a daily basis. My desire to share information on my native country and the chance to respond to children's curiosity about my dog's breed, prompted me to write this book. Please enjoy and learn.

Available to all bookstores nationwide.
www.publishamerica.com

also available from publishamerica
THE COCKAMAMY WORLD OF A. YOLD
by Paul Mackan

I first met A. Yold in the dumps. I was down there for—well, that's for another time. Two guys meet in the dumps, they're Canadian, they talk! It's a national characteristic. "Strangers in the night?" Not if they're one of us. Now I am one kind of Canadian; Yold is his kind. Anyway, thinking seasonally, I said, "Are you having a happy Easter?"

"Easter-shmeester," he said. "I'm a Jew." It was the start of our friendship.

It felt funny addressing him as "A" all the time, but he wouldn't tell me what name the initial stood for. All he'd say was, "So you should hear it from me; my mother is unorthodox." And after a pause, while I couldn't think of a thing to say, he lowered his head and smiled. "She's the original Hadassa bizarre." And I was in love—do not infer.

Paperback, 81 pages
6" x 9"
ISBN 1-60610-055-6

About the author:

Paul Mackan lives in Ottawa, Ontario. He's an award-winning writer, broadcaster, and film maker. He's the widower of Sara Lee (Harris) Stadelman, to whom he remains single-mindedly committed. He does film and stage work, and is a member of both Alliance of Canadian Television and Radio Artists, and Canadian Actors' Equity.

available to all bookstores nationwide.
www.publishamerica.com

also available from publishamerica
WHY I AM A COUNSELOR
by Anthony A.M. Pearson

Why I Am a Counselor is a powerful and painful story about a little boy's journey into the darkness and what he learned. It is about overcoming, persevering, discovering purpose, and about liberation and success! Inspiring all who have heard it, it is a true story about a spiritual-psychological awakening that brought about an empowered, authentic life. It explores the questions:
• What forces can take a sickly, fearful, abused child and empower him to become a minister, teacher, and counselor of excellence?
• What is a counselor, and what was the journey that led the author to become a counselor?
• What beneficial life lessons can be drawn from the myriads of counseling theories?
• Can a spiritual-psychological collaboration benefit human existence and the counseling profession?
• How do humans reach maximum potential?   The author hopes that this self-revelation will inspire others to make their own journeys, overcome challenges, and understand their purpose in life.

Paperback, 133 pages
5.5" x 8.5"
ISBN 1-4241-9186-6

About the author:

Anthony A.M. Pearson is an ordained minister, educator, counselor, teacher, historian and motivational speaker. He was trained in theology, history, and counseling psychology. He is married, with five sons and nine grandchildren. A recipient of numerous honors and recognitions, he is founder of **Winds of Change Institute**, a human-potential organization.

available to all bookstores nationwide.
www.publishamerica.com

also available from publishamerica

THE 1776 SCROLL
By Louise Harris

Living alone in Philadelphia, 19-year-old Charlie Schofield struggles to repair the shattered relationships in her life while fighting for her spot in the Magical Strike Force Academy. She takes up with a lonely friend who secretly knows that Charlie is in danger. An evil wizard plots against Charlie over powerful magic locked in a scroll. When Charlie cannot open the scroll to release the magic, the wizard hatches a new plan to discredit her in court using more conventional means: she's to prove herself insane and the scroll a hoax. Will Charlie unlock the magic in the scroll before the wizard goes free? Will she prove that she was the victim and not the perpetrator of a crime? Or will the court decide that she is nothing more than an attention-grabbing witch? It is a race against outer forces and inner demons.

Paperback, 104 pages
6" x 9"
ISBN 1-4241-5098-1

About the author:

Louise Harris aspired to write since her youth. She published her first poem at age 12, wrote her first song at age eight, and became an editor. *The 1776 Scroll* is her first novel. Louise lives in Arizona with her husband, three children and two cats. Her heart remains in Philly.

available to all bookstores nationwide.
www.publishamerica.com

also available from publishamerica
THE HEART DONOR
By Nick Wastnage

When a terrorist group linked to al-Qaeda threaten to target London with a nuclear device, three people, with separate agendas, are thrown together in a scary countdown to a world crisis.

Jake Armstrong, investigating an art theft, wants to know who's got his wife's heart. She died after being caught up in a terrorist explosion and he agreed to her heart being donated.

Becky Rackley, an MI5 agent, received a new heart after rheumatic fever rendered her own heart useless. She meets Jake at a party and comes away believing she's the recipient of his wife's heart—as does Jake, but neither have discussed it.

Paperback, 234 pages
6" x 9"
ISBN 1-4241-7878-9

Grigoriy Nabutov, head of the largest Russian organised crime group, plans the heist of a futurist Russian painting. It fails, and he's forced to bargain with Chechen terrorists seeking high-enriched uranium. A world catastrophe looms, London's evacuated and Jake stares death in the face.

About the author:

Nick Wastnage, once a Royal Marine, shot in a skirmish with terrorists in Borneo, was a retailer before becoming a thriller writer. He was born in East Anglia, England, and lives with his wife and family in Buckinghamshire. *The Heart Donor* is his fifth book.

available to all bookstores nationwide.
www.publishamerica.com